A Paper SNOWFLAKE Christmas

A Paper SNOWFLAKE Christmas

MADDIE EVANS

Philangelus Press
Boston, MA

ISBN: 978-1-942133-53-7
Cover art by Christina Murphy of Paper or Pixels
Editing by Julie Monette

Two Weeks Before Christmas

Text Exchange

Jazz: Christmas time! What will you be doing?

Marlie: Nothing.

Jazz: Seriously? Nothing.

Marlie: Seriously, nothing. My parents have a destination wedding in Hawaii, and since Santa isn't bringing me a plane ticket, I'm not going.

Jazz: Rude. Who even has a destination wedding on Christmas? Can you hang out with your brother?

Marlie: My brother is going, too.

Jazz: And your parents won't pay?

Marlie: They say I'm the one who at age twenty-five has a career that doesn't pay for me to fly out to Hawaii for Christmas.
Marlie: Anyhow, what are you doing?

Jazz: Well, until a minute ago, I was going to Vermont

to be with my parents.

Marlie: Ron's still on a ship in the Pacific?

Jazz: That's the Navy for you. Although maybe I can have him storm the beach wedding and send your family home.

Marlie: Thoughtful of you, but it's a cruise ship.

Jazz: Okay, so new plan. You and me and ten friends rent a ski lodge. We hang out by a fireplace and tell ghost stories and make Christmas dinner.
Jazz: You can make personalized origami ornaments for everyone so we always remember.

Marlie: Nice idea, but no one's going to come.

Jazz: I'm posting it now.

Marlie: You're what? Wait!
Marlie: Why did you just blow up the Fun Cool People group chat?
Marlie: I'll be fine. I'm planning to stay in Bangor and work on the syllabus for the spring semester.

Jazz: You can do that from a ski lodge, too.
Jazz: Meanwhile, plans are taking shape. Gorgeous plans. Christmas plans.

CHAPTER ONE

Marlie's phone hadn't stopped buzzing all day.

Once Jazz got an idea, you'd have a better chance smacking a cannonball out of the air with a fly swatter than changing her mind. The only thing to do was wait for the idea to die on the vine as every one of the Fun Cool People replied that they were heading for Lewiston or Manchester or Providence, and, therefore, they couldn't come.

Which, to be fair, did happen with most people. But Bri had agreed to go in on it. Jazz was already changing all her plans with her parents. (They were probably used to it. Maybe they'd show up at the ski lodge, too.)

The Fun Cool People group chat was another of Jazz's ideas that had started out as a means of keeping in touch with their high school best friends but afterward expanded to include many people who were neither best friends nor had gone to Hartwell High School. Marlie had long since decided Jazz's categorizations were as fuzzy as they needed to be, and she did recruit fun people to the group.

...All of whom now knew Marlie was the kind of person whose family didn't want to include her at Christmas.

Marlie would have been fine staying home. Her apartment was a slice of the first floor of a converted Victorian, none of the rooms square nor the floor quite on-level, and yet cozy. If she wanted, she could buy a tiny tree for the living room and decorate with origami cranes. In fact, she'd done almost exactly that last year for the local rehab hospital, teaching a group of residents how to fold simple stars and cubes, the paper coming from a copy of *A Christmas Carol* that had been discarded by the local library.

It wouldn't exactly be pathetic to do that on her own, right? Put on a movie, bake some cookies, and fold a bunch of shapes to stick in the branches.

The phone buzzed again, and Marlie glanced at the screen, then did a double take.

Devin: "Mom says you can all come here."

Devin?

Devin Supple?

Before Marlie could finish blinking, Jazz had already texted, "DEVIN? You're still alive?"

The group chat blew up. Apparently everyone else thought he'd blocked them all. Marlie had figured Devin had quietly left the chat, kind of the way he'd periodically left everyone's life and then popped back in again as though he'd never gone.

Except it didn't feel that way to Marlie. He'd vanish, and she'd miss him, and then he'd return for a few months. After she'd gotten used to him being around, he'd vanish again.

One of the guys said, "I figured you'd gone to prison."

Devin replied, "Very funny. The house has four bedrooms and a finished basement. There's a Christmas tree, and there's a fireplace."

Come on, Jazz. Ask him. Ask him.

Marlie huddled on the couch, knees to her chest. Jazz was darned near telepathic. She'd know what Marlie wanted to know. She'd want to know it, too.

Jazz finally did it: "Where have you been?"

Devin replied, "Hartwell. You don't need to act like I've risen from the dead. Marlie needs a place to go. I've just volunteered a place."

Was he still living at home, then? For that matter, did he even have a home? Because the last time Marlie had heard anything about Devin, none of it had been good. Not quite "rock bottom," but digging.

Jazz said, "Would your mom even be okay with this?"

Of course she would. Mrs. Supple had always been more than okay.

Devin replied, "It's her idea."

Jazz texted with enough emojis to turn a text message into a shriek. "Then we're doing this!"

A moment after came a flurry of short texts. Jazz would bring movies. Bri would bring popcorn. Marlie only needed to bring herself (although of course she'd bring more).

Marlie finally tapped the window to type, "And Devin—you'll be there?"

Especially now? Especially after his latest disappearing act? It felt vital to be sure.

Devin replied, "Yes. I'll be there, too."

CHAPTER TWO

Marlie automatically turned off the state route onto the wrong street because her subconscious mind was heading back to her childhood home. It took two turns to get back on the right road, but that was how this whole Christmas was going to go, wasn't it?

She'd prompted Mom with a text to learn if they'd landed yet. Mom hadn't replied, meaning either Mom's phone was in airplane mode, or Mom herself was in airplane mode. There would likely be photos coming at some point, photos of Mom and Dad on the deck of a ship where her mom's college roommate's daughter would be getting married to the love of her life. They'd mingle while holding champagne flutes. "Oh, Marlie's teaching three classes next year at two different universities," they'd say. Who knew? Maybe when the other guests said, "What subject?" between the two them, her parents could cobble together an idea of what it was.

Meanwhile, Devin's mom not only knew enough about

Devin's life to know what was going on in a group chat he hadn't participated in for six months, but also, she'd opened her home to as many strangers as wanted to crash there for Christmas.

Mrs. Supple had always been like that. Devin was the oldest of three, his sisters one and two years younger than him (and, honestly, with such a firebrand being the first, it was a surprise that the younger two even existed). On Devin's first day of kindergarten, for example, this wiry, curly-haired student immediately delighted the teacher by climbing the bookshelves, then scaling the windows up to the ten-foot-high classroom ceiling, finally popping off the screen so he could leap outside.

Marlie had stood, face to the glass, watching her classmate lead the staff on laps around the schoolyard until her teacher had called all the children away from the window. Half an hour later, Mrs. Supple had led in a sweaty, bedraggled Devin by the hand and made him apologize to the teacher.

He'd said it wearing the biggest grin. Devin was not sorry.

Marlie wasn't sorry, either. Mrs. Supple had remained in the classroom to help for the rest of the day, and Mrs. Supple had been very nice during circle time and snack time and stations. When it had been Marlie's turn for the fishtank station, Devin had blurted out an entire essay about how to care for fish and how Mrs. Merritt's fishtank lacked merit (hah). Marlie watched him the whole time, and every day, he kept making her laugh. Within a week, possibly because Mrs. Merrit couldn't stand the daily harassment, the fish had upgraded their home to a twenty gallon tank with a heater and a filter and bright pink substrate.

All of this to say, Devin Supple had been a rogue even at age five, and Anita Supple was a saint.

When Marlie pulled into the driveway, Saint Anita stepped outside and waved her toward the side entrance. She looked a lot older than the last time Marlie had seen her, or maybe just wearier. She'd cut her hair shorter, and it was shot through with silver.

Woodsmoke scent filled the air as Marlie hefted her bag from the back seat, and then she walked past Jazz's sedan and an SUV she didn't recognize.

Inside, the house smelled of onion and chicken. "Was the drive bad?" said Mrs. Supple, as though Marlie had driven from Bangor, Michigan rather than Bangor, Maine.

"It was fine. Only about forty-five minutes." She shifted her weight. "Thank you for having us here, Mrs. Supple."

"Call me Anita," she corrected.

Marlie looked around for a place to put her stuff, but then Jazz bounded into the room with her ponytail swinging. "Oh my goodness, you look great! I'm so jealous of all you people who get rosy cheeks when it's cold as opposed to me, looking like I got attacked by a snowman." Before Marlie could even get her breath to reply, Jazz said, "Leave your bags here because you have got to see something amazing right this second!"

This was the same house Marlie had known twenty years ago, updated only a little. The appliances were mostly the same, and so was the carpet, and the furniture had changed by becoming more worn. The basement steps leading off the kitchen had been redone, though, and the lights were brighter. At the bottom of the steps, she turned —and stared.

Too much, all at once. The basement had transformed into an apartment. Finished walls, finished floors, and even its own kitchenette. From the base of the steps, Marlie could identify a bathroom and a bedroom door, plus a wide space with a couch and a massive television—and in the center of the room, Devin.

Holding a curly-haired child.

Jazz clasped her hands. "This is Cory, Devin's nephew! Isn't he adorable?"

At the word "adorable," Cory's entire demeanor changed. He went from cautious to posing for the camera like a runway model. Marlie laughed.

Devin flashed her a smile, his angular face transforming with that mischievous expression that always captivated her as a kid. His dark hair and dark eyebrows gave his face a sharp expression that, as he held his nephew, made him look protective.

Marlie said, "Your nephew—Alyssa's son, or Rachel's?"

Devin said, "Neither, anymore. I'll tell you later." He set Cory on the floor, and Cory returned to a couch covered in die-cast metal cars. "It's been a time."

Jazz said, "They said we could all crash in the guest bedrooms, but given the adorableness, we could set up shop down here in Devin's apartment and let Cory hold court."

Marlie flinched. "I don't want to take your apartment."

Devin gestured to Cory. "You'd be the first person concerned about that."

His voice had that same rough edge as it did in high school, not quite a growl but rather a low vibration that gave his words a perpetual sardonic grade. It gave Marlie shivers.

Jazz mock-sighed. "Well, she's right. You've been nice about us staying, so having us invade your apartment would be rude."

Upstairs, there was one bedroom for Anita and another for Cory, plus the bedrooms that used to belong to Alyssa and Rachel. "We'll share," Jazz declared while claiming the larger guest room, and that declaration of one massive Christmas sleepover was the end of all discussion. She assigned Marlie to the bed and unpacked an air mattress. "When Bri comes, she'll bring her own air mattress."

Marlie, Bri, and Jazz in one room, giggling well past midnight, would no doubt thrill the saintly Mrs. Supple. Maybe they should have taken the basement. Maybe Devin could have hidden in Cory's room to escape.

Marlie breathed, "What's the deal with Cory?"

Jazz stepped closer. "Devin had the kid with him the whole time, so I didn't want to ask, but it sounds bad. I don't think Devin's sister died, but maybe she abandoned the kid?"

"Knock knock!" Bri appeared in the doorway, still wearing gloves and a wool cap over her short blonde hair. "I hear we're having a sleepover in this room! Plus, Anita has cooked enough for an entire regiment."

Jazz hugged her. "Everyone's here! Now we're all tucked in for the holiday."

Marlie raised her eyebrows. "Tucked in?"

"You know what I mean. Everyone's in the house." She turned to Bri. "You have to meet Cory. He's downstairs with Devin, and he's the cutest thing ever."

Bri raised her eyebrows. "Is he single?"

Marlie said, "He's four years old."

Bri frowned. "I'll have to pass. That'd be a bit of an age

16

gap." She dropped her bag on the floor. "Anything else I should know about? Like the other spare bedroom is for Santa?"

Jazz extended her hands. "Of course. And six of his reindeer!"

Marlie put her arms around Jazz and Bri. "Thank you guys for putting this together for me. I'm glad to be with you for Christmas, even if we have to room with the reindeer."

CHAPTER THREE

After an amazing dinner, the three guests cleaned the kitchen while Cory watched a Christmas cartoon in front of the TV. Devin hadn't said much during dinner, and he didn't say much now, taking the dishes Marlie dried and putting them in whichever cabinets they called home.

She offered, "Everyone sets up their kitchen differently. It's hard to know where to put things."

Devin shrugged. "You put things where they make sense or where they fit."

His voice gave her shivers, but there wasn't enough of it. He didn't add anything, didn't follow up. He had that kitchenette downstairs. Surely he could have said, "I had a hard time figuring out where to put the cereal bowls," or "Plastic container lids never fit well anywhere," but instead in silence he took dry serving bowls from Marlie's hands.

When they joined Cory in front of the TV, Jazz plopped herself right at his side. "I liked watching this special as a kid."

Cory regarded her with suspicion, then slid off the couch and climbed onto Devin's lap.

Jazz slumped against the couch. "Wow. Putting me in my place."

Marlie tucked up her knees and said, "Hush. This is the best part."

A moment later, she noticed Cory staring at her, wonder in his brown eyes. She rummaged around in her head for what might have attracted his attention, then said, "Is this your favorite part, too?"

He nodded big, then returned to the screen with intent.

Bantering with Jazz felt natural. Marlie hadn't thought twice before firing a quip back at her. But as far as Cory was concerned, Marlie had just defended him, and that had surprised him. What had the kid even been through?

After the cartoon ended, Anita took Cory to get his bath. Devin stood as if he was about to exit the room when Marlie blurted out, "Why is he living with you?"

Devin sorted through the remotes to turn off the TV. "He's Rachel's kid. We practically never saw her or him, but last January, out of the blue, she asked Mom to babysit for the weekend. Well, sure, right? At least we'd get to see him at all. She dropped him off with pajamas and a few toys. Then Sunday night comes, and no Rachel. She wasn't answering her phone, wasn't anywhere we could find. Eventually, we got the landlord to open the apartment, and she'd gone."

Marlie put her hands over her mouth.

Devin's eyes darkened. "I don't know what her problem was. We managed to track her down, and long story short, she signed papers, and now Cory is Mom's kid."

Marlie swallowed hard. "And now you have a little

brother."

Devin's mouth twitched. "It looks that way, right?"

Jazz said, "Well, it sounds like, legally, it is."

"Rachel doesn't even care." Devin huffed. "Mom was done with kids. Once everyone was gone, she was home free, planning to sell this place and move somewhere smaller, maybe even go somewhere warmer."

Marlie offered, "I can't believe anyone would want to leave all this lovely snow."

"Now, she can't." Devin turned to her quickly. "And don't try to defend Rachel. If I saw her right now, I'm not sure what I'd do. A lot of yelling would be involved, and I'd have to have another uncomfortable meeting with my probation officer."

Marlie raised her hands. What she said was, "I'm not defending Rachel."

What she thought was, *Your probation officer?*

Jazz, who normally blurted out the things Marlie wouldn't dare ask, only said, "I'm not defending her, either. Cory's really sweet."

Devin glanced off to the side. "Must take after his grandmother."

Marlie ventured, "Maybe he takes after his uncle?"

Devin glowered. "No one has ever mistaken me for sweet."

Anita emerged from the hallway, and Devin sighed. "I'm sorry," she said, but he was already on his way down the hall. As he left, Anita said to the girls, "Cory's very attached to Devin. He wants Devin to give him his bath and put him to bed."

Marlie turned aside. "Devin said no one's ever mistaken him for sweet—but that's very sweet."

Jazz said to Anita, "How could Rachel just abandon him?"

Anita looked weary. "I don't know what got into her—or rather, I suspect I do know what got into her. Whether by injection or pill or smoking it, that's still up in the air." Her hands clenched. "Cory's safe, and that's the best I can do for now. I hate that I had no idea she'd been neglecting him. He never even had a real Christmas before."

Bri tucked up her knees. "That's hard. I'd be so angry."

Anita glanced back up the hall. "Devin's been a lifesaver. He moved back to help with Cory. We finished off the downstairs as an apartment so he could have some privacy, but he's hardly ever in it. Between me and Devin, working different shifts, Cory's got someone with him all the time."

Devin had mentioned working second shift. "I didn't realize he'd chosen that schedule to help with childcare," Marlie said.

Of course, Devin also hadn't said there was a child. At no point in any of their texting had he talked about his sister's little boy, who seemed to have become his own little boy.

"I couldn't do it without him." Anita sighed. "On the one hand, I feel bad that he's giving up years that he should be spending on his own life, but then on the other hand—"

She cut herself off, and again Marlie's proverbial antennae went up.

"On the other hand."

"His probation officer."

Back in the kitchen, Jazz had her phone out and was looking up activities she'd planned for the days until Christmas. The holiday stroll! The lights at the town park! The Santa Parade! Decorating a Christmas tree! Through it all, though, Marlie couldn't concentrate on the details of who would shop for Christmas dinner because she found herself tangled up in the things Devin wasn't saying.

In middle school, Devin had always been able to make Marlie laugh. He was so unlike her brother and unlike her father, very much larger than life. He'd been the one to scale the school walls to retrieve tennis balls that got stuck in the window safety grates, and then he'd been the one to laugh when the teachers shrieked in dismay. He'd gotten his driver's license as soon as possible, and then he'd been the first of Marlie's friends to wrap his car around a tree because he didn't believe you needed to slow down in the rain.

In fact, he'd been the first to drive a car at all—by about eight years.

Devin always lived life outside the margins. The same way he hadn't colored inside the lines in kindergarten, colors had bled outside the lines of every part of his life. His laughter had been louder, his jokes funnier, his insights sharper. At every turn, there just seemed to be more of Devin than the world could contain.

Except then Marlie had gone to college, and Devin had stayed behind. There hadn't been a choice. Marlie's parents had sent her to Middlebury, and then she'd gone on for graduate school. Her parents had moved out of Hartwell, so she'd never come back again.

Everyone from high school had scattered. The "cool people" chat group started by Jazz remained the silver thread connecting them all.

Bri handed a paper to Marlie. "Anything else?"

On the paper was written:

- *Ham*
- *Potatoes au gratin*

- *Sulad*
- *Rolls*
- *Cranberry sauce*

Anita said, "What makes the holiday special for you? I want to make sure we make it."

Abruptly, Marlie felt as at sea as her parents' cruise ship. What made the holiday special for her? When she sat down at the table, what needed to be there, otherwise the holiday just wasn't complete?

With a nervous laugh, Marlie shrugged. "There isn't really anything."

Jazz huffed. "Come on. We're all here because your parents ditched you. Let's at least make you feel at home."

She looked around at all the faces. Anita Supple, who'd opened her home. Jazz, who'd organized the getaway. Bri, who showed her care in her careful planning. And in the doorway, Devin, holding a damp, tousle-haired boy in fleece pajamas who looked sleepy but warm.

"Lights," Marlie said. "Christmas lights make the holiday special for me. You don't need to do anything special, though, because you've already made me feel at home."

CHAPTER FOUR

While Jazz and Bri worked out three days' worth of menus, Marlie accompanied Devin to Cory's bedroom.

Putting Cory to bed, Marlie discovered, was not a matter of tucking him in and making sure the teddy bear was in the right spot. First there were the stories, which Cory insisted Marlie read. They all got under one of the extra blankets, sitting the wrong way around on the bed, backs against the chilly wall. She read first one story, then another, and when Cory begged for a third, Devin told him no, absolutely no. Then came the songs, which Marlie didn't know. (Cory kept telling her, "but it's the goodnight song!" and couldn't believe how his urgency didn't restore it to her memory.)

Following the goodnight song, Devin arranged a half dozen stuffed animals, then tucked a stuffed dragon under the covers. Following that came one more goodnight song. This one Marlie was familiar with, so she sang it, too.

Cory's nose wrinkled. "You could have sung the other

one."

Devin said, "Don't be rude."

Cory huddled under the blankets. "I'm sorry, Miss Marlie."

She patted his shoulder. "Tomorrow, I want you to teach me the whole goodnight song, that way, when it's time for bed, I can sing it to you."

Devin turned on a small lamp in the corner and only then shut off the main light. He didn't close the door, but instead sat in the hallway.

Marlie sat alongside him. "We sit guard for a while, like watchdogs?"

"Something." Devin pitched his voice really low, like a breath. "I don't have to stay in the room anymore, but he wants me near until he's asleep."

Marlie murmured, "It must have been hard for him."

"You've got no idea." He gestured down the hall. "You don't have to stay. It's usually about fifteen minutes."

Marlie went into the guest room and dug in her bag until she found her origami paper, then rejoined Devin in the hall. He was reading something on his phone as she settled alongside him. While he watched, she pulled off the sheet of paper at the top of the stack, then started folding.

Devin smiled. "You still do that?"

"I'm surprised that you remember." Fold. Crease. Flip. Crease. Flip back. She worked the paper, rubbing it against her laptop like a makeshift desk. In a minute, she finished with the final pulls, and she handed Devin a paper crane, saying, "O flock of cranes, protect this child."

Devin took it, pivoting it in his fingertips. "Does it work? Will a whole flock of cranes flutter in the window if I'm about to put Cory's right shoe on his left foot?"

"Absolutely. If you wake up and find an entire flock of cranes standing in the yard, you'll definitely want to make sure he's okay." She grinned. "Or maybe it has nothing to do with anything."

He handed it back, but she said, "You can keep it."

He gave a mischievous grin and narrowed his eyes. "You didn't write anything inside it."

Marlie stiffened. "You remember that, too?"

"I remember everything." He leaned forward. They were already so close because they needed to whisper, and now they were within inches. She should have felt the heat of his breath. "I remember you folding giving me one of little cubes and telling me they all had messages inside."

Marlie's heart hammered. "And do you remember the message?"

Here Devin faltered, and nausea overtook Marlie. The message. He hadn't thought this through. He should have pretended he'd forgotten.

He handed her the crane. "I never opened it."

He had to be lying. The way he'd responded—he'd looked inside. He'd been embarrassed. And then he'd tried to pretend it never happened.

Kind of like her parents. They also pretended she'd never happened. It was better that way.

Marlie said, "Well, I'd probably write something lame in this one, too. I'll save us both some trouble and leave it blank."

He gestured toward Cory's room. "If you give him one, can you write something inside? Then teach him how to fold it back up again, that way he can keep it."

Best to run with the change of subject. "Would he like that?"

"He seems attached to you. If you can give him something special, he would hold onto it."

She swallowed hard. "Won't that make it harder on him when we all leave?"

"He knows you're guests. But maybe." He sighed. "I'm way out of my depth. Like, I thought I knew about kids. I was a kid, so how hard could it be? Turns out, it's wicked hard."

Marlie chuckled. "Being a kid isn't good practice for raising one."

"Thank goodness Mom had experience because she knew right away all the things we had to do. Me? I'd have barely figured out we needed to feed him, let alone that he needed therapy and an assessment from the early intervention people. She hit the ground running." Devin hesitated. "You guys were talking about Christmas dinner. It might end up being dinosaur nuggets."

"If Mr. Cory requires dinosaur nuggets in order to be happy, then dinosaur nuggets he shall have." She patted Devin's leg, then felt blisteringly self-conscious. "I wish you'd told us about him. It was kind of a surprise."

"I didn't want you to think..." He stopped. "It's an awkward situation. Once you saw him, I knew you'd be okay with him. But I didn't want you to write off my whole family as a mess, not without seeing us."

Marlie huffed. "I don't deserve my own family. Do you really think I'd turn up my nose at yours?"

"That's not true, but I didn't want you to stay away. He's such a good kid."

Marlie squeezed Devin's hand. "He is a good kid. I wouldn't have stayed away."

Still, she would have brought Cory a Christmas gift.

Tomorrow, she'd have to find at least some time to go shopping. The adults had all agreed not to buy gifts for one another, but Cory had made no such agreement.

She pulled out another paper, then hesitated. "What would I write in it?"

Devin didn't answer.

He must be remembering what she'd written before.

Ten years before.

In a little yellow cube.

Don't answer. Don't answer that.

He didn't answer. Not at first.

As Marlie resumed folding the paper, he said, "What do you usually write inside the origami?"

Her hands trembled. "It's supposed to be like a fortune."

Devin's nose wrinkled. "Most fortune cookies don't give you a fortune. They give you an aphorism."

"That bugs me, too. A fortune cookie should say, 'Trust your friends,' not, 'A great friend is trustworthy in great things.'"

Devin said, "How about, 'Don't forget your ID when checking into a hotel'?"

Marlie's nose wrinkled. "Leave an extra twenty minutes for traffic."

Devin said, "Bring your umbrella."

Marlie said, "There will be a surprise when you go visiting for Christmas."

Devin nodded. "That would have been helpful for you, but then you would have asked me what the surprise was."

"And you would have informed me," Marlie shot back, "that revealing the surprise would make it not a surprise. So there."

Devin struggled not to laugh.

Cory emerged from his bedroom, frowning. "You're talking too much."

Devin handed Cory the paper crane. "Maybe it wasn't us talking. Maybe it was the paper crane talking."

Cory stuck it in Devin's face, then squawked, "Be quiet." Next he pointed it at Marlie. "You, too."

Devin's voice dropped in tone. "Don't be rude."

Cory dropped the crane and stepped back. "I'm sorry! I'm sorry!"

Marlie passed the crane back to him. "Why don't you take this to bed with you, and if we talk again, you can send him out to tell us to be quiet?"

Cory took it at arm's length, then fled into his room. Devin heaved himself up off the floor to tuck Cory back in.

Devin stayed in the room while Marlie sat in the hallway, folding paper, creasing it, unfolding it, and then folding back across the markers, forming birds that never would fly.

CHAPTER FIVE

On the morning of the 23rd, Marlie awoke, and she listened to the house. On an air mattress by the windows, Bri's deep breaths meant she was deep in sleep, but Jazz had already left. Marlie pulled a hoodie over her flannel pajamas and headed to the kitchen, where she found Jazz eating a muffin while Cory shoveled cereal up with a spoon.

"Hi, Miss Marlie," Cory garbled out, with the predictable admonishment from Anita not to talk with his mouth full. He worked hard to swallow quickly, then repeated it.

Marlie said, "And good morning to you, too, Mr. Cory."

Anita showed her the coffee and an assortment of breakfast pastries. "One of the benefits of Devin working at the nursing home is he brings us the morning pastries they'd otherwise be discarding."

Jazz raised her muffin. "Eat up, Marlie, before it goes bad!"

"Not like that." Anita grinned. "And he doesn't hover over the elderly residents, admonishing them against taking seconds. 'You're taking food out of my nephew's mouth.'"

Glancing over the selection, Marlie said, "Does he make all these?"

Anita shook her head. "They're shipped in, and the morning crew sets them out. Before two o'clock, anything not eaten is supposed to go in the dumpster. Except, of course, no one does, and that's when the staff descends on them."

Marlie said, "Devin didn't tell us about his job yesterday."

"Second shift, runs the dining hall at the Willowgate Assisted Living Community. You probably won't see him before ten o'clock in the morning because he stays on that schedule."

Jazz said, "I never imagined Devin cooking."

"They had a program to bring him up to speed." Anita paused, uncomfortable. "When he needed a second- or third-shift position so we could trade off taking care of Cory, they were already there and waiting for him."

Marlie said, "So is he making their Christmas dinner?"

"Unfortunately, he's junior man on staff, so he can't get the day off. We'll eat our Christmas dinner early so he can get theirs ready. "

Jazz smirked. "So rude, all two hundred residents wanting to eat even though it's Christmas."

Marlie poured some coffee. "And they'll probably want him to clean up afterward, too."

"He also runs room service until 10 p.m. After that, it's teardown and closing duties." Anita shook her head. "He's off for tonight, but he's on for Christmas Eve, when they're going to have a party for the residents. We're invited to that."

Cory sat up taller. "They want me to come."

Marlie nodded at him. "Of course they want you to come. I bet you make everyone smile."

He said, "If I ask anyone for a quarter, they'll just give it to me."

"Cory!" Anita turned. "You don't."

Cory grinned as he crammed more food into his mouth and chewed slowly so he didn't have to answer.

Marlie said, "If you're jingling when we walk out of there, I'm going to know it's not Santa's reindeer we're hearing."

Jazz said, "Dasher, Dancer, Prancer, Swindler."

Anita huffed. "You'd better not be doing that."

Cory just looked mischievous. Marlie chose a lemon pastry and sat at the table. "What would you buy with all that money?"

Cory sounded abruptly serious. ""I'd give it to Grandma. Food is expensive."

"Don't worry about money." Anita leaned against the counter. "You don't have to support the family. Devin and I earn enough that you can have food and clothing."

Cory didn't look convinced.

Marlie said, "Did your paper crane keep you safe last night?"

Cory's eyes widened, and he knocked over his chair as he bolted down the hall.

Jazz picked up the chair. "Is that, no, the crane didn't keep him safe? Or, yes, the crane kept him so safe that it deserves a reward?"

A minute later, Cory returned to the kitchen, eyes watery as he held the crane out to Marlie. "I'm sorry. I'm so sorry.

I forgot him. He's all crushed."

Marlie took the bird. "I bet we can get him in good shape again."

Jazz sad, "Or you could make him another. It's just paper."

Cory sniffled. Marlie said, "It's not just paper, but he'll be fine."

She opened up the bird and smoothed some of the wrinkles, then said to Cory, "Do you have a pencil?"

When he shook his head, Anita handed one to Marlie, who drew a smiling face on the back of the paper. She showed it to Cory, then re-folded the paper crane. It was a little wobbly when she was done, and his wing had a crease she couldn't work out, but overall, the bird looked good. She presented it back to Cory, who took it at arm's length.

"I can make your crane a friend, if you like," Marlie added, and Cory thought about it for a while before agreeing.

Cory finished his cereal while Marlie folded and creased.

Jazz announced, "So, on the docket for today—we're buying a Christmas tree! And then we get to decorate it."

Anita said, "I'll need help getting the ornaments from the crawlspace."

Jazz said, "Since Devin's around until after lunch, we'll be able to get the tree set up. After he leaves, we should do something fun for dinner and maybe watch Christmas movies."

Anita said, "Tomorrow is the party, and Cory—you can get your picture taken with Santa."

Cory's nose wrinkled. "Why?"

Anita said, "So you can tell him what you want for Christmas."

"Oh." Cory picked up his paper crane. "I want this paper crane."

"Fortunately for you, you've already got that paper crane." Marlie leaned forward and winked. "And in a little while, you can have a second paper crane."

Cory said, "Did you write a secret message inside this one, too?"

Marlie flipped over the paper and drew a tiny Christmas tree with a star on top. "Now, I have."

Cory stood beside her, again looking serious. "Good. Because everyone has a secret inside."

Chapter Six

Jazz's anticipation of Christmas movies in the afternoon became Christmas cartoons in the morning as Cory planted himself in front of the television. Marlie and Anita went into the crawlspace to retrieve the boxes of ornaments.

Anita said, "Thank you for coming and making the holiday special. Cory never had a Christmas tree before."

"That's sad." Marlie dragged back the first box. "I didn't realize things had gotten that dire. He was worried about money during breakfast."

"You saw how scared he got when he thought he'd ruined the paper crane. I have him in therapy, but sometimes I wonder what's lurking behind those eyes." Anita sighed. "Between Devin and Rachel, I wasn't sure what I'd do, but then Cory arrived, and Devin turned himself around."

Marlie lowered her voice. "Devin mentioned a probation officer."

"Yeah." She deflated a bit. "He's doing so much better now, though, and it's all because of Cory. I would never want one child's self-destruction to prompt the redemption of the other, but that's how it played out."

Marlie took the box Anita pulled out of the crawlspace, and all she said was, "You'd have been there for them both."

"I would have, but there's not enough of me to go around." Anita's voice sounded plaintive. She dragged out the second box. "I think this is it for ornaments. Devin already put up our outside lights, at least. He didn't want to be doing it if it snowed this week."

Marlie said, "Besides, they're pretty. The lights are my favorite thing about Christmas."

Anita turned to her. "Oh! We have to make sure you get to the park for the light display." Anita paused. "I'm not sure if Cory will like it because I haven't been there for a few years. It's possible it's very kid-friendly, but, you know how it is. He could get bored and spend the entire time whining."

Marlie chuckled. "Cory doesn't seem like a whiner. He's a little drill sergeant."

"You get that impression, too?" Anita laughed. "He has his routines and the things he expects to happen, and heaven help you if you don't get them done to his specifications."

Remembering Cory scolding her last night for talking too loudly, Marlie said, "Devin wasn't like that."

Anita chuckled. "Devin was exactly like that, except not with rigidity. For him, it was always about the potential of a thing. He wanted to be able to do what was right, not necessarily what was correct."

Marlie grinned. "Wow, it's almost as if you raised him."

From behind, Devin's voice sounded amused. "Are you

dragging my name through the mud again?"

Anita said, "Exactly the way I always do. Here, carry these into the living room."

Devin stepped around Marlie, leaving her skin tingling with his presence. He was wearing jeans and a flannel shirt, but he still seemed sleepy. "Sorry I slept in."

Marlie said, "You needed the sleep to help us get the tree up."

He hefted a box. "Saving all four damsels in distress, no doubt." And he snorted a laugh.

Marlie followed him into the living room with the other box. Still watching TV, Cory ignored Devin setting down the box.

Marlie said, "To be fair, a tree is heavy."

Devin straightened up, making his shoulders look even broader than before. "It's no match for me." Then, with a grin, he returned to normal. "I'd like to say we're hiking into the woods to find the perfect sapling, but we're just going to Main Street to pick one out in the parking lot of the hardware store."

"A hundred pound tree is a hundred pound tree."

"I doubt these come in at over sixty pounds, but point taken." He picked up a paper crane off the coffee table. "I see the bird invasion has continued."

Marlie nodded. "Flocks of them. I don't think they trust me."

"What's the deal with these, anyhow?" Devin pivoted it in his hand. "I hear things like, the legend of a hundred paper cranes. What's the significance?"

"The idea is that if you make a thousand paper cranes, your wish will come true." Marlie lowered her voice so she wouldn't disturb Cory in front of the TV. "But I think they're really about patience and waiting. It takes a while to make each crane, so to make a thousand, you have to be pretty determined. I'm going to bet that if you're determined enough to make a thousand paper cranes, you're probably doing other things to make your wish come true, as well."

Devin handed it back. "That would tend to stack the odds in your favor."

She arched her eyebrows. "Right? So which came first—the legend, or the stubbornness?"

Devin winked at her. "Are you stubborn? How many thousands of paper cranes have you made?"

She replaced the crane on the coffee table. "I haven't kept count."

Devin tugged one of the end tables toward the far wall. "How will you know when your wish is supposed to come true?"

Marlie hesitated. "What am I wishing for?"

"You've got to be wishing for something." Devin stood and went for the opposite end table. "Everyone has wishes."

"Not everyone has a wish. I'm happy as I am." When Devin looked disbelieving, Marlie added, "I've got it pretty good."

"Except for your whole family abandoning you."

"I don't have the kind of money to hop on a plane for a Christmas wedding." Marlie shrugged. "That's hardly their fault."

"That's entirely their fault." He huffed. "Who even does that?"

"They do that. It's fine." Marlie crinkled her eyes at him. "Besides, how would Santa find me out on the ocean?"

"He's certainly not finding you here." Devin opened his hands. "You and Jazz insisted no Christmas presents, so unless you left cookies by the fireplace in your apartment, Santa's GPS isn't tracking you."

"My landlord looks askance at tenants who set fire to the building, alas. No chimney. No cookies."

Devin's nose wrinkled. "Help me move the couch so we have a place to put the tree."

Marlie moved to the opposite side of the couch. "Wow, making me lift furniture. I thought I was the damsel in distress."

He snickered. "Damsel in this-dress. You've got to listen carefully before you agree to these things."

They got the couch over near the wall, and then Devin stood back. "Lights," he murmured. "We should string lights."

Marlie lowered her gaze. He was saying that for her.

Devin glanced around the whole room. "Strings of lights for the walls and windows." He stepped toward her, beaming. "Let's string up a thousand of them."

CHAPTER SEVEN

With so much to be done, Anita assigned everyone tasks. Despite Devin's insistence on buying thousands of lights, or perhaps because of it, Anita put Bri and Jazz in charge of obtaining a few more lights, the garlands, and a bunch of Christmas stockings. She planned on going to the grocery store with Marlie, and Devin would buy the tree with Cory.

This worked until the moment Cory attached himself to Marlie's leg. "I want to stay with Miss Marlie."

Anita said, "I thought you wanted to get the tree!"

Cory had, it seemed, two disparate wants: he must stay with Marlie, and he must pick out the tree. Thus, a change in plans: Marlie would buy the tree with Devin and Cory.

"You've seen grocery stores in Bangor," Anita said, stifling laughter. "You're not missing out on much."

Devin would drive the SUV out to the hardware store. Cory sat in a booster in the back, and he demanded Marlie sit in the back as well. "This is going amazingly," Devin muttered darkly. "Much more of this and you'll think Cory runs the house."

"What's the harm?" Marlie winked at Cory, who giggled. "Unless the back half of the car is going in a different direction than the front half, we'll all get there. You'll just arrive half a second sooner."

Devin glanced at her through the rear-view mirror. "And if the back half of the car did go somewhere else, I guess Cory would need an adult with him anyhow."

Hartwell had more traffic now than it had when Marlie arrived, but she suspected Christmas Eve would be the worst in terms of traffic. The streets weren't exactly straight, nor were all the intersections at right angles to one another. You got used to it after you'd been there a while—or in Marlie's case, she'd never had to get used to it because she'd grown up here. But after being in bigger cities, she'd begun seeing the benefit of laying everything out on a grid.

The air was brittle, and the windows, frosty. Devin cranked up the heat, and Marlie settled back in the seat, letting her scarf protect her neck and chin. Cory wore a puffy jacket, a hat, and mittens. Although they hadn't had snow, the temperatures were just right for it. The dry air begged to differ. They might get snow on Christmas, but now the sky had a crystal brightness, and the sun cast sharp shadows that belied the temperature.

"Hartware" was no longer called Hartware. The original owner of the Hartwell hardware store had sold it to another owner who'd sold it to a franchise that had (showing excellent taste) changed its name to something that didn't make newcomers spit out their coffee. Of course, the locals hadn't changed the name they used in conversation, but that was to be expected because it had only been ten years.

As Marlie unbuckled Cory, she said, "Do people still say Coffee Corner instead of whatever it got changed to?"

Devin frowned. "Wait—it did get changed, didn't it?"

The coffee shop had changed ownership and changed names before Marlie was born. Hartwell residents just had really long memories. Either that, or else "set in one's ways" was the highest form of praise they could think of.

Or both.

The tree-picking process was desperately exciting. "This one!" Cory would shout, then run up to the next and, surprisingly, ("This one!") that tree was even better than the previous one.

"If you're curious," Devin murmured, "and I'm sure you aren't, this is why we opted against a hike in the forest."

Marlie smothered a laugh.

In an equally low voice, Devin added, "How many trees shall I bring home?"

Marlie said, "All of them."

He nodded. "That may be the most logical choice."

Indeed, Cory loved them all. They were big and wonderful and perfect, and he wanted to give their tree a name, and he wanted the best tree ever. Devin tried to apologize to the attendant, who waved them off. "This is the part of the job I like best," he said. "Let your son run himself ragged a bit."

Marlie didn't correct him. It didn't harm anyone if just for this moment, they were a tiny family.

After Cory stopped pinging from tree to tree like a pinball lighting up all the bumpers, the attendant rejoined them. "Do you want to know a secret about Christmas trees? Some of them are healthier than others."

The attendant then showed Cory how to pick a healthy tree. He showed him how to run his hands over a branch to make sure the needles weren't falling off, and how to check for nice green needles. He had him tug a few branches to make sure they wouldn't snap. "Here, I'll show you a sick tree," he said, and he brought Cory to a tree with a lot of brown needles off to the side. "We can't sell this one because a family like yours needs a healthy tree."

Cory frowned. "You need a tree doctor."

The tree was more than a little past the point of benefitting from a tree doctor, but Devin said, "That's a good idea. He'll call a tree doctor, but the next thing we need to figure out is how tall a tree we need for our house."

Cory spread his arms. "I want the biggest tree!"

Marlie said, "The biggest tree would have to go right out the roof!"

Cory shrieked as though that were the funniest idea ever. He bounced and talked about branches going out the windows and having to slide down a tree to get downstairs to Devin's room, and by the time they were with the seven-foot trees, he was running in circles around as many trees as he could. Devin walked through at a much more sedate pace, checking for roundness and color. Marlie kept inhaling the pine scent. "It's got to smell good," she explained. "If it doesn't smell good, it's not going to be healthy."

Devin carried Cory to a cluster of trees and showed him four that might be good choices. "Miss Marlie wants a tree that smells nice, so I need you to smell these and tell me which is the best."

Cory stuck his head into all the trees, one at a time, and solemnly inhaled.

Marlie said, "It doesn't really have to be—"

Devin said, "You expressed a preference. I hear and obey."

"Scented pine and a thousand lights." Marlie tilted her head as she looked at him. "What am I, the queen?"

He sized her up. "Maybe the princess."

"I can deal with that. And you—"

"I've always wanted to be an archduke. I have no idea what dukes do, but whatever it is, an archduke does it archly." When Marlie snickered, he called out, "Cory? Which one?"

Cory pointed to the third of the four. "This one is the smelliest!"

"Quite the endorsement." Biting his lip so he wouldn't laugh, Devin turned to the attendant. "One smelly grand fir, please."

The credit card swipe went fast. Much slower was the process of feeding the tree through the netting machine. "It's getting dressed," Cory whispered to Marlie, then giggled. He tried to climb Devin, who hefted him up, and then with his head resting on Devin's shoulder, he watched the attendant saw off the tip of the stump.

Cory said, "I want one of those."

Marlie said, "We're getting the tree."

Cory said, "The saw. I want a saw."

The attendant grinned at Devin. "Tell your son he can come back in about thirteen years, and I'll hire him on the spot."

Devin shifted Cory on his hip. "The last thing the world needs is Cory wielding a chain saw," and Marlie turned away so Cory didn't see her expression.

The last step of the process was tying the tree onto the

roof of the SUV, which Cory also found incredibly silly. "There's a tree on the roof!" he kept giggling, but he was fading fast. The last of his energy wore off as they pulled out of the Hartware lot, and before they were out of town, Cory lay slack, his head lolling to the side.

Marlie was seated in the back again. "He's gone."

"Yeah, I figured he'd be like a sack of potatoes once we finished. That's good, though. Keeps him out of trouble."

Marlie smiled at the sleeping face. "He looks so innocent. What trouble could he possibly be?" and when Devin spat, "Hah!" she smothered a laugh.

"Oh, feel free to laugh," Devin added. "I could drive us into a wall, and he wouldn't wake up."

"I'd prefer you didn't."

"Yeah, it wouldn't look good on my record."

For a moment, the only sound was the humming of the engine.

Finally, Marlie said, "Can I ask—?"

Devin didn't meet her eyes in the mirror. "Sure, you can ask. The charge was criminal mischief, which you have to admit fits me like a T."

Marlie glanced out the window. "I'd have to check our yearbook, but I don't think you were voted most likely to be arrested for criminal mischief."

"Do you remember Michelle Parsons? She had a job over at the fast food place at 186 and Main, except her manager was a toad." Devin's fist clenched the wheel. "The first day she was working, everyone warned her not to let the manager trap her in the walk-in because he had this habit of feeling up the female staff where there weren't any cameras."

Marlie shook her head. "So everyone warns her, and

everyone knows it, but no one can do anything about it?"

"See," Devin said, "Michelle failed to mention to anyone that she was a black belt. After she found one of the sixteen-year-olds crying because the manager caught her alone, she put herself in a place where she'd be able to get in a little good old-fashioned self-defense. He approached her from behind, so she flipped him over her shoulder and planted him on his back. Gave him a concussion and broke his wrist. No cameras back there, remember? So, oops, her word against his—except suddenly every employee wanted to talk to the cops about this guy."

Marlie said, "And I'd say he got off with a slap on the wrist, except his wrist was already in a cast."

"Good one." Devin grimaced. "The owner was the manager's friend, which is how he managed to stick it out so long there. Anyone who talked to the cops got retaliated against, in all sorts of miserable ways. Michelle needed the job, and before she could find another one, the owner was cutting her to like two hours a week."

Marlie's mouth twitched. "Constructive dismissal."

"You can't prove it with these jobs. Sure, he'd have crew members working close until after midnight and opening again at six-thirty, and others pulling doubles all weekend while Michelle was only working from one to three on Thursdays, but it's all fungible. Staffing is a hard thing to prove in court, and anyhow, who has the money?"

"Fair enough."

Devin said, "What doesn't take a lot of money is getting drunk out of your mind with your friends and finding the owner's car, slashing the tires, and keying the blazes out of it."

Marlie flinched. "Yeah, that's affordable."

"The most expensive part was the beer. Afterward, you get assigned the public defender, so that's free. Of course, he then informs you there were video cameras that caught you in the area. It's kind of circumstantial. They *might* be able to get you off. But also, you *might* get convicted of a felony, and you might get jail time. So you plea down to a misdemeanor and probation and an alcohol program, and meanwhile, the grapevine ensures that everyone in the town knows to avoid that particular fast food. The place is practically dead now. I give it another six months before they're closed."

Marlie said, "Did Michelle get a better job?"

"Yeah. It was long enough after that it seemed, at least while I was drunk, that they might not connect us to it." He hesitated. "I was the only one. We were all at a party where we were egging each other on to find the best revenge, but I was the only one stupid enough to go out and do it."

Cory was still asleep, so Marlie said, "If you'd been sober, you'd have come up with something so much better."

He paused, then shook his head. "You're right, and that scares me, which is why I went for the plea. I'd rather have someone looking over my shoulder so it doesn't escalate to where someone winds up dead."

Marlie said, "Or you."

"It's Cory." He glanced in the mirror, but Cory was still unconscious. "Rachel lit out while all this was going on, and it was bad. He used to wake up in the night screaming, so I'd sleep on his floor because he was so scared of being alone. His mom's all messed up, and who knows if she'll end up dead or in prison? He didn't need me to end up dead or in prison, too. I needed to get my life together for him."

Marlie whispered, "That's amazing."

"It's hardly amazing. You do what you have to do." He glowered. "You had your priorities in order and didn't take twenty years to figure yourself out. Mom says I took the scenic route. Cory can't take the scenic route. We need him on the straight and narrow path right from the start."

Devin's father had gone to prison. Anita had divorced him while he was serving his time, and when he'd gotten released, he'd left the state. No one had heard from him since.

Devin went on, "So now I had to be here for a kid, and I had no idea how you'd even do that, except I figure it started by getting a job and not getting felony-levels of drunk. The probation program made sure about the second part, but the job? Well, it turns out they wanted me to be gainfully employed, and they hooked me up with a kitchen job."

Marlie forced a smile. "Where you don't get groped, one assumes?"

"Some of those residents? You gotta be careful." Devin looked mischievous. "A number of them have memory issues and a limited brain-to-mouth filter, so I keep my distance. But you know? It's a good job, and I'd like to stay there long term. I get to set the menus, and they gave me a say in how the kitchen got renovated, and sometimes I get to sit with the residents when they ask for stuff made to order outside the regular meal times. They tell me all sorts of stories."

Marlie said, "That does sound neat."

"There's a lot of time compacted into that one dining hall. Tons of memories." He started. "Sorry, you don't want to hear about that."

"I do want to hear about that. I never got to sit with my grandparents and listen to them tell me stories."

His face softened. "A few of them have adopted me as an honorary grandson. I have one grandfather who has told me his smoked brisket technique a dozen times, so we're going to have to bring out a smoker sometime and do it while he lectures me a thirteenth time. I've gotten a few handknit scarves, too."

Marlie looked down. "They care a lot about you."

"They'd care about anyone who cooked for them." His mouth twitched. "I bring Cory sometimes, and he gets a month's worth of attention in a couple of hours. They all demanded I bring him to the Christmas party tomorrow, so he's got to come."

Marlie said, "Are the rest of us invited?"

"Of course. I've got nineteen grandparents who will swear before a judge and six CNAs that you are their granddaughter what's-her-name who's driven here from Tennessee just to visit." His eyes crinkled. "I made sure each of you got written in on someone's guest list." He hesitated. "Some of them didn't have guests. It's sad. So maybe it's a good thing I messed up so badly, that way some people end up happier."

CHAPTER EIGHT

Cory awoke while Devin was trying to get him out of the booster seat. Anita, Jazz, and Bri weren't back yet, so Marlie and Devin wrestled the tree into the living room by themselves while Cory insisted he could help, and then they managed to get it into the tree stand without it toppling over. Also without getting a massive headache from Cory shrieking.

"Little dude!" Devin exclaimed. "Santa's going to hear you all the way from the North Pole!"

Cory crawled under the tree getting the skirt around the stand, and then Devin filled the stand with water. They found and tested strands of lights from the boxes, then started winding them onto the branches.

"We need at least another ten strings of light," Devin said, starting at the bottom.

"It isn't Christmas until you turn on the tree, and the entire town loses power." Sitting on the opposite side of the tree, Marlie took a coil of lights from him and worked it around the bottom on her side.

At the back of the tree, she passed it toward Devin. His hand touched hers, and she went warm.

"The bigger the fire hazard, the better the holiday." Devin worked carefully, tucking the wires in the branches. "They say not to attach more than three strings of lights to one another, but that's just cowardice."

Marlie said, "Behold. I am a chicken."

Devin leaned around the base of the tree to hand her the lights again, and he looked right into her eyes "Bwuk bwuck."

"Totally me." She didn't inch back right away. "Don't get me wrong. I'd like to sit in front of a roaring fire on Christmas Eve—but contained in the woodstove."

He leaned toward her. "You don't like when things get too hot?"

That felt almost—sparky. She took the lights and darted back behind the branches.

Cory had abandoned them, of course. He had the attention span of a preschooler (unsurprising) and had disappeared into his room to play. Talking in the car, without Cory awake to hear, seemed to have loosened up Devin. As she brought the lights around toward him, though, he dialed back down a notch. "Santa's in red, and the fire fighters are in red—but I guess that's where the similarities end."

"We could leave out raw cookie dough for the firefighters, and then when the tree ignites, they'll have warm, fresh cookies."

"With a sweet glazing of fire retardant foam! Just like Grandmom used to make every time she set fire to her oven." Devin reached around the tree again to pass Marlie the lights. "Would you care to enjoy a sweet, palm-sized grease fire?"

Marlie tried to sound serious. "Snickerdoodle flambé—delicious." Devin was back to normal, at least. That flirty tone must have been an aberration.

"All kidding aside," Devin said, "do you remember those strings of lights with the big bulbs? My grandparents used those. Every year, they'd drag out the same thick cord of lights they'd used since Gerald Ford was president, and they'd assign us kids to screwing in the bulbs and making sure everything lit up."

Draping the thinner cord over the branches, Marlie said, "Screwing in the bulbs?"

"After Christmas, they'd unscrew them all. I have no idea why they thought storing the lights that way would preserve them."

Marlie sent the lights back around. They were running low. They'd need the second strand attached soon. "The lights lasted fifty years, so don't laugh."

Devin continued laying lights on the branches. "The thing was, those bulbs got *hot*. As in, burn-your-hands hot. So Granddad would have the string plugged in, and you'd be screwing in a light slowly until the moment it flared on, and then you'd screw it the rest of the way as fast as possible so you didn't burn your fingertips. Also, heaven forbid you put two of the same color next to one another. Grandmom would make us take them out again and reshuffle to get a more even distribution."

Marlie knelt up while Devin plugged the next strand in to the first. As it lit, she said, "I'm surprised you still have fingerprints."

"I'm surprised we're alive at all, especially when they

kept forgetting to water the tree, so the thing was dry as a matchstick and those bulbs were burning five hundred degrees." He snorted. "If you're wondering where I got some of those jokes about the Christmas fire hazard—well, they go way back."

His hands touched hers again as he passed the second strand of lights around the back of the tree. She arose from her knees, and when she passed it around the back, he was standing, as well.

This time he definitely touched her hand as he took the lights. "You can see why I want better for Cory."

Okay, so had she flipped a switch with him? Was the pine scent doing something to his brain? If he'd come on to her like this in high school, she'd have died on the spot.

That is to say, she'd have passed notes all through the next class saying, "I died on the spot," detailing every single thing he'd said, every move, every expression, ending with, "What do you think? Does he like me?"

He sent the lights around to her, and she wished Jazz were here to pass a note to. *Does he like me?*

Devin in high school had been so much larger than life. In high school, if someone's Christmas tree had burst into flames, it would have been Devin's. Devin would have been the one who brought a plate of blackened flame-retardant cookies into the homeroom class and spun them like Frisbees to random classmates. It would have been Devin who slid along the bench of the cafeteria table, pulling up just short of bumping Marlie, and then opened his lunch to hand her a blue Christmas bulb.

She took the string. "At the top of the tree, I assume your grandparents had an actual lit candle?"

"For Pete's sake, what do you take them for?" Devin

rolled his eyes. "They'd never allow wax on the carpet. We had a butane lighter."

She giggled. "Not the acetylene torch?"

He deepened his voice. "I'm afraid the restraining order prevented my Granddad from owning an acetylene torch."

"Now there's a story." The lights were circling the tree faster toward the top, so she barely had time to get to the front before he was passing the lights to her. "You know those Fourth of July sparklers we used to light up?"

"Oh, we used to do 'Christmas Crackers,' too. I wish you hadn't made me remember them." He grinned devilishly. "I think they were tubes filled with gunpowder, and you'd pull them apart and they'd go bang, and you'd get to keep whatever gift was inside, assuming it survived."

This time, behind the tree, Marlie didn't let go of the lights right away. "That's why you said no presents for Christmas? Because you hate wrapping gifts in gunpowder?"

He pitched his voice lower to match hers. "It adds to the surprise if you only wrap *some* of the gifts in gunpowder."

She kept her hand on the lights. "You'll need to warn me before I open anything, then."

He said, "Just for you," and she let go of the lights.

At the front of the tree, Devin held out the lights, but, like Marlie, didn't let them go. He said, "Just in case you weren't joking, the whole point of 'no presents' was that having you all here was the present."

Okay, he was serious again. She changed her tone. "It was nice of you to host me. And—" she interrupted as he drew breath to interrupt her, creating something of a recursive interruption, "—don't you dare tell me you're hosting *us*. I'm the only one who needed a place to go."

Devin's nose wrinkled. "Well..."

"You knew I didn't have any money because money is the reason I didn't fly to the wedding." She tilted her head. "Hence the no-present rule. You arranged everything around me. I noticed that."

He released the lights. "It's not that much trouble."

Something in his voice drew Marlie up short. Not the words. The words were exactly as one would expect after you put someone to an immense amount of trouble. Instead, it was his tone that unsettled her, as though the whole rigamarole of spare beds and extra place settings wasn't the trouble he meant, and she hadn't nailed down the actual trouble.

She took her time with these lights, and when she passed them back, she thrust them at him with no banter.

With the tree blocking their line of sight, Devin said, "Yes. The idea was to give you a place to stay and not cost you a lot of money."

He handed her the lights. She said, "Thank you."

Her voice was tentative.

The lights had climbed to nearly the treetop, and Marlie struggled to get them into the branches. In an attempt to lighten the mood, she said, "I also appreciate that nothing will explode, catch fire, or otherwise demolish all of Maine."

He took the light strand. "For once."

"I'm not the one who set fire to the chemistry lab."

Handing back the light coil, he said, "Technically speaking, I wasn't, either."

Marlie stretched, but the lights had finally gotten high enough that she needed to stand on something to reach the top branches. And then behind her she felt Devin standing, reaching, taking the lights the few extra inches from her hands and getting them hung.

He had her between him and the tree. She stepped toward the windows so he could get around her, but instead he followed, face inches from hers. Her body tingled as though her nerves were strung with lights. His eyes gazed into hers, and she stood, tall, hesitant, waiting.

Jazz, do you think he likes me?

In a dusky voice, he said, "Somethings, things just spark."

Marlie pitched her voice to match. "If the fuel is there, it goes right up."

He braced the hand holding the lights on the window, and he leaned toward her. "The question is whether it's supposed to catch like that, or if you want it to."

She swallowed hard.

He added, "If you don't want that chemical reaction, then you say something, and you pull those two things away from each other."

Marlie's mouth was dry, her stomach tight, her hands clenched. The window at her neck was a chill at odds with the heat before her and the lights at her shoulder.

Did she want this spark?

Did she—

Devin slammed into her then, knocking her into the window. He exclaimed, "Cory!" while Cory laughed loud and sharp.

"Lights on the tree!" he shrieked. "You didn't tell me you were putting lights on the tree."

"You nearly knocked Miss Marlie out the window, you human cruise missile." Devin sounded irritated, but was he disappointed? Because Marlie had no idea what she was feeling, and it seemed almost easier to work out what Devin was feeling than herself.

Cory said, "Oh!" and looked around Devin's legs. "I'm sorry, Miss Marlie!"

Devin helped Marlie step out from behind the tree, hand on her forearm. Cory was pointing to the lights still in Devin's hands. "Can we finish? Can you lift me up, and I'll put on the lights!"

Devin stepped away from her to pick up the boy, and then from the kitchen, Anita called, "Can I get some help with the groceries?"

Any sparks had faded out in the winter air. Marlie went to the kitchen without looking over her shoulder at Devin.

CHAPTER NINE

Devin would have to leave for work at 1:30, so they'd have time for lunch. "Christmas dinner will be complicated, so today it's easy stuff, just sandwiches," said Anita.

Devin added, "Christmas Eve dinner will be at the facility, so that should be easy, too. At least, easy for you guys."

Marlie said, "You'll be working the whole time?"

"Yep. Don't expect a tour of the kitchen." He looked at her mischievously. "Unless you want to report for closing at ten p.m. and help with the deep clean."

She opened her hands. "I've used bleach before!"

"Bring your galoshes for when I mop the floor." He glanced at his mother. "Mom thinks this is hilarious, by the way. I was the worst kid on earth for chores, so now I get to do them on a regular basis."

Anita said, "We'll have to decorate the tree tomorrow morning, though, because there probably isn't enough time to do it before Devin leaves."

Cory let out a whine.

Devin said, "Little dude! Is that how we ask for things?"

Cory pouted. "I want to do it today. Please."

Marlie said to Devin, "He did say please."

"Yeah, but wild horses had to drag it out of him." Devin looked to his mother. "Having said that, I'm a grown-up, and if I don't decorate the tree, my Christmas won't be ruined."

When Cory bounced in his seat, Anita relented. "Well...it probably would make things easier to get it done this afternoon."

Cory was all over the place while they cleaned up: *Is it time to decorate the tree now? When is five minutes from now? Can we do it yet?*

Eventually Marlie said, "Hey, come here."

She brought Cory to the table with a stack of origami paper, her real scissors, and Cory's safety scissors. "Have you ever made a snowflake?"

When Cory said he hadn't, Marlie folded one of the square papers into a stacked series of triangles. "Let's start snipping and see what happens."

Using the sharp scissors, Marlie cut multiple notches in the triangles. With the paper folded up like this, she struggled to imagine what it would look like all stretched out. Some people could do truly fantastic work with their papercrafts, but hers only needed to entertain a preschooler, so she tried not to worry too much about the final product. As long as the end result looked like a snowflake, Cory would like it.

If it looked terrible, well, then any snowflake Cory made would look better by comparison. Win-win.

Marlie gathered the tiny cut-out pieces into a pile, then

unfolded the paper snowflake before Cory. When he gasped, it was with the joy of a child who'd just opened up a whole new area of learning.

Anita dropped some plain paper on the table. "Maybe don't use your good origami paper on this."

Suddenly serious, Cory nodded. "Snowflakes should be white. Your paper has colors."

Fair enough. Marlie showed Cory how to fold one corner of the paper over and then cut the remainder off so it became a square. Then she demonstrated how to fold triangles, over and over. One snip to get the point off left them with a long triangle. "Now you make cuts where you want the snowflake to be snowy. Just make sure you don't cut so much it falls apart."

Cory worked with his safety scissors while Marlie prepared another triangle. When he'd hacked the poor thing to pieces, he unfolded it with shrieks of laughter.

Devin said, "Little Man, keep it to a dull roar."

He held it aloft and dropped it on his head. "It's snowing." Then he snatched up the second triangle. "I want to make a blizzard."

To make a blizzard might require more paper than the federal government used in six months, but Marlie got to work making more triangles. One of his snowflakes fell apart, but rather than getting upset, he just moved on to the next.

Devin sat across the table from Marlie and followed her motions to make his own triangle. "Okay, now, how do I do this?"

She winked at him. "You've made these. I was there in second grade when they taught everyone."

He grimaced. "As if I remember anything from second

grade."

Marlie held up her triangle. "Cut some notches, and don't cut up the sides. The idea is, it needs to all unfold as one piece, and any shape you want needs to be bisected. It's going to open out into its full self, but until then, you're only going to see it as half."

Devin hesitated, and then, "You make it sound mystical. We only see our half of a situation until it unfolds, and then the design is revealed because of what isn't there."

Marlie squinted at him and tilted her head.

He said, "Well?"

Marlie began, "That's—"

From the sink, Anita said, "That's life."

Marlie added, "I guess we do only know the parts we can see. Sometimes the full bit never unfolds, and we have to figure it out based on what we think is folded up underneath."

Cory opened his snowflake, nothing like a real design because he was cutting at random. "I want another!"

Marlie passed him hers, then traced lines on a new triangle. Here, the spine of the triangle. Here, the base. Here, off the end. Here, up the sides. She snipped a few times until there was almost nothing left of the original.

Devin said, "How's that going to work?"

Saying nothing, Marlie opened the paper to reveal a six-pointed star with frost prongs jutting out between them. "Like this."

Devin's eyes widened. "I take it back. That worked."

She said, "You can make them look like flowers or like traditional snowflakes. Some people make them three-dimensional." She handed the scissors across the table. "Let's see what you can make."

"Not what you made," he muttered.

He did the snowflake equivalent of off-roading, cutting notches into the paper, making certain to leave the base intact as well as the sides. He was also cautious, which was terribly cute. "It's only paper," Marlie reassured.

"It's not only paper," Cory breathed, hacking into his triangle. "It's snow."

Jazz came up behind Marlie. "It's magic."

Devin finished snipping away the piece he wanted to, then unfolded the snowflake. It had jagged edges, getting wider toward the base. He extended it to her. "What do you think?"

Tingling, Marlie said, "Each prong looks like a Christmas tree."

A Christmas tree, with the two of them tucked up against the window, lights in their hands and the scent of a great fir leaving her intoxicated with the aura of magic.

A Christmas tree—where anything could have happened. Until the moment Cory happened.

"At least you recognized my attempt." He stood from the table, leaving Marlie to wonder what he'd intended to do behind the tree. "I need to get ready to leave. Cory, I want enough snow to make a snowman by the time I get home."

Cory snickered, and Marlie watched Devin withdraw from the kitchen.

Jazz took his place, then reached for a triangle. "He's being a good sport."

Marlie managed, "Yeah, he is," wondering what sport this might be, and if anyone knew the rules.

CHAPTER TEN

When you want to know the rules, you ask the better players.

Jazz had already gotten married, so Marlie took it on faith that Jazz knew about relationships. Although Bri wasn't dating anyone at the moment, she had always been reliable to figure out the behind-the-scenes details in high school and college.

When Anita went to bed at nine-thirty, Jazz put on a movie (softly, with subtitles) in the living room before the decorated tree, then tucked up on the couch with a throw blanket over her legs and her phone in her hands. "Sometimes Ron's available all night, and we can text," she said, wistful.

Marlie said, "It must be hard. You should be together."

"I knew what we were signing up for. Well, what he signed up for. It's just that when you get married, you're effectively saying, 'Did you sign up for that? Then I'm signing up for it, too.'"

Bri was also scrolling her phone. "I couldn't become a military wife. It's not for everyone."

Jazz offered a painful laugh. "Yeah, they don't have online support groups for wives of bakery chefs."

That was an opening, but before Marlie could take it, Jazz continued, "What's the deal with you and Devin?"

She'd kept her voice low, but it stabbed through Marlie's heart. Marlie said, "I was going to ask you."

Bri said, "I didn't plan to ask anyone anything," and Jazz bopped her with a throw pillow.

Marlie giggled. "I mean—do you think he likes me? Because I'm confused."

"Oh, come on. You were totally carrying a torch for him in high school. I'm surprised the whole tree didn't light up with the afterglow." Jazz rolled her eyes. "I thought he was flirting with you a few times, but you always shut him down, and I never understood that."

Marlie swallowed hard.

Bri said, "I saw the way he was looking at you when you were making paper snowflakes. If you're confused, I think he's trying to figure you out, too."

Jazz got a dreamy look. "It's Christmas, and it's perfect. We just need to arrange for a light snowfall and a cuddle in front of the fire, and it's a done deal."

Thinking of Devin's joke about setting fire to the Christmas tree, Marlie said, "That's the question, though. What deal does he want? Was he looking like he couldn't figure out why I was even in his house?"

Marlie scooted closer to the couch. As both her friends set down their phones, she tried to relate what had happened while lighting the tree, only the thoughts kept getting jumbled up. He'd been joking with her. Cory wasn't around. He'd touched her hand a few times. And then he'd had her trapped against the wall—no, not trapped. More like he'd enclosed himself with her in a small space, a very small space, and she'd wondered how much smaller it could get when it all felt like something so much bigger.

Jazz sighed. "And then the kid ruined it."

Marlie muttered, "Pretty sure I ruined it first."

Bri said, "If you'd put your arms around his neck and kissed him, that would given you your answer."

Jazz brightened up. "What's the worst that could happen?"

Marlie snorted. "We're here for Christmas. The worst that could happen is everything gets horribly awkward and we repay Anita's generosity by ruining the holiday."

Bri sat up. "Oh! Do I finally get to throw a glass of wine on someone?"

Jazz nodded with enthusiasm. "Someone has to end up in tears. Let's draw straws."

"I can't end up in tears because I'll be the one who stalks into my room and slams the door, packs my things, and storms out to the car only to realize Devin parked me in." Marlie opened her hands. "What do you think? Should the cops come, or would that make it too festive?"

Bri said in a low voice, "I've got some relatives where the cops probably phone the night before to ask when the drinking's going to start, for scheduling purposes."

"In my family, the fire marshal rings the bell and asks what time we intend to have dinner. Same reason." Jazz tucked up her knees. "Okay, so that's the worst case scenario. What's the best that could happen?"

Marlie furrowed her brow.

Bri said, "Ah, you've given this no thought whatsoever."

Marlie's mouth twitched. "It never occurred to me that there's also a best case scenario."

"If there's one end of the pole, there's also the other." Bri shifted on the couch. "What do you want to happen? In the best case scenario, you get that, and also, the police don't come."

Jazz looked at the ceiling. "In the best case scenario, you get that snowfall and the cuddle in front of the fire. He kisses you in the light of the tree and says you're the Christmas present he's wanted all along."

Marlie said, "And then what?"

Bri opened her hands. "And then happily ever after?"

"It's not..." Marlie lowered her voice. "Okay, so, back in grammar school, long before any of us were setting fire to Christmas trees, my parents talked to Anita at the school play. They were already annoyed because I was playing one of the crowd members and in one scene I got to act as someone's writing desk, and that was my on-stage debut rather than as a coloratura soprano. They talked about nothing on the way home other than how low-class the Supple family was, with the father in prison and the siblings running wild after school."

Jazz rolled her eyes. "How *dare* Anita work to support her family?"

Bri added, "Shocking."

"They made like they were going to have me removed from Devin's class because, I don't know, he was going to influence me to skip Volunteer Beach Cleanup Day in favor of robbing a bank." Marlie pursed her lips. "They never forgot that, and they'd never accept him."

Bri sat back. "Sounds like they have issues."

Jazz said, "My parents flipped their lids when I decided

to get married to Ron. They hated that we were young and really hated that he was in the Navy. Like, I think they could have maybe tolerated if he was Air Force, but Navy? But after they got to know him, they accepted him, and now they even like him."

"You know my parents. In the same situation as yours, they'd be on the phone with me every week to tell me horrible stories about men in uniform and mailing me business cards for a nice divorce attorney."

Bri murmured, "Which they'd expect you to pay for."

Marlie sighed. "That's not even a question. They've got long memories and hold longstanding grudges."

Jazz said, "You're way ahead of yourself. If you kiss him in front of the Christmas tree, that's not a marriage contract."

Bri shook her head. "It's smart to know how far you want to take things. If Marlie wouldn't go all the way to marriage, then why start?"

Jazz said, "Because sometimes, it's fun just to start. You can go for a jog without intending to run the Berlin Marathon. I studied literature in college without aiming for a PhD."

Bri looked at Marlie. "Devin is a fun guy. He might not want to settle down, either. You don't know until you ask."

Marlie shook her head. "I never thought flings were fun. I'd fall for him and want to commit, and then I wouldn't be able to."

Jazz said, "Unless you could."

Marlie tilted her head.

"You're not five years old. You don't need Mommy and Daddy's permission to date someone." She leaned forward, chest to her tucked-up knees. "They're not paying for your life." Granted—otherwise Marlie would be on the deck of a cruise ship, not talking about a guy she'd crushed on for twelve years.

Marlie said, "They'll be disappointed."

Bri shrugged. "They've been disappointed before."

Jazz snorted a laugh.

Marlie only shook her head. "You don't know what they're like. Not really." The subtle comments, the insults you couldn't quite make out, their assertion that you were "too sensitive" when you objected to anything, the snubs, and always—always—the ways you weren't quite good enough.

Marlie's brother had managed to clear the bar and become good enough. She'd heard over and over about her brother's successful career. *Oh, the house is amazing. You have to see it sometime. He just got a new car. He's going on a trip to Munich!* And then if Marlie tried to talk about her own life, thjey'd change the subject because a one-bedroom apartment and a ten-year-old car just weren't as interesting.

She'd be inviting Devin into that dynamic. After twenty-five years of feeling like he hadn't been good enough for his own father to stick around, Devin could then feel like he wasn't good enough for his parents-in-law, either. How could that be fair?

Frankly, it would be the biggest act of love for Marlie never to marry someone she actually cared about.

Jazz said, "Maybe we don't know what your parents are like, but we do know what you're like. And if you want to ramp things up with Devin, I think you should see where they go. You're a good person, and you deserve someone who loves you."

CHAPTER ELEVEN

At nearly midnight, an engine sounded in the driveway, followed by the thump of a car door. Shortly, Devin came inside.

Marlie looked up from the coffee table where she sat behind stacks of paper cranes. At her side, Jazz yawned. Bri had turned in an hour ago.

Marlie said, "How was work?"

"Demanding." At the counter, Devin set down a box, presumably tomorrow morning's pastries. "It's nice to come home to a lit house, but I'm surprised you're still awake." He bent to lift a paper crane from the coffee table. "You've been busy."

Jazz said, "She's phenomenal."

Marlie said, "It was something to do while watching the movie."

Devin said, "What did you watch?"

All normal conversation. If Jazz was hoping for a sparkling romantic soliloquy to emerge from either of them, she was about to experience Christmas disappointment. Instead of sticking around, though, Jazz dropped her throw blanket over Marlie's shoulders. "I'll see you in the morning."

Marlie replied after her as she disappeared up the hall, "I'm probably not staying up much later, either."

Devin said, "Thirty more minutes, and it'll be Christmas Eve." He hesitated. "Do you want some hot chocolate?"

That might be a bid to spend time with her alone. Cory was unlikely to crash into them while he was sound asleep.

Marlie said, "You've been cooking all day."

Devin said, "It's okay. I'm a bit cold, so I was planning on making it."

"I didn't say no." She must have looked like it, though, while puzzling things through. "I was just thinking that Cory might wake up and beg for some."

"He's a little stinker. He's got radar for candy and anything else you don't want him to find." Devin stepped into the kitchen, and Marlie followed, the blanket around her shoulders and a half-done paper crane in her fingers.

At the kitchen table, she finished the crane, then folded a new snowflake triangle while Devin got out the sauce pan. "After working in a kitchen for ten hours, you should make me do it."

Devin smirked. "You're a lot more pleasant to cook for, and you can take me at my word on that. For one thing, I doubt you keep an instant-read digital thermometer in the pocket of your housecoat to stick into anything I set before you—"

"No!" Marlie exclaimed.

"—and then complain when the temperature isn't whatever magic number you've pulled out of thin air." He straightened. "Wait. Please don't tell me you have a digital thermometer in your pocket."

"I'm fresh out of thermometers." Marlie shook her head as she traced curvy lines on the snowflake triangle. "Dial it forty years into the future, though, and you're describing my mother."

"Thank heaven you aren't in possession of either a thermometer or your mother's perspective." He exaggerated a motion of wiping sweat from his brow. "I can heat milk in perfect confidence."

Marlie sighed. Her mother. Her father. They'd be the terror of a care home or the terror of their home health attendants, or, most likely, the terror of her because she'd be the one who had to take them into her house when the time came.

It hurt thinking about that. Marlie started cutting her snowflake.

The silence must have lingered too long because Devin said, "Sorry. I'm not really conversational after work."

"It's fine. I'm tired, and I didn't even feed two thousand people."

Brows arched, he looked at her over his shoulder. "Slightly fewer than two thousand."

She snipped off one of the shaded snowflake bits. "And that's after you put in, effectively, a full day's work putting up the tree."

He smiled reflexively, as though just the thought of picking out the tree and stringing the lights was a memory that surprised him with joy.

Would you have kissed me? The more Marlie thought about it, the more she thought, yes, he would have. And what would it have been like? Would he have kissed her quickly and with a laugh? Or would he have drawn up against her slowly and lingered, his mouth soft, his facial hair prickly against her chin, his scent mingling with the pine as she closed her eyes and longed to remain forever in that moment?

His attention returned to the stove where he turned down the heat and stirred in the cocoa powder, then added a little vanilla. "I like dolling it up a bit," he explained. "Also, to be completely transparent, this is hot *cocoa*, not hot chocolate. I didn't begin with real chocolate and then thin it down with milk."

Marlie grinned. He still had his back turned, so she opened out the snowflake to reveal she'd created an array of hearts. Oops. She folded it back up again. "I appreciate your honesty. Is it acceptable if I enjoy it anyhow?"

He poured cocoa into the waiting mugs. "If you can overcome the crashing disappointment, sure."

Marlie said, "You've never disappointed me."

The words were out before she thought about what she was saying. Devin hesitated mid-step, then set down the mugs. "Never?"

Leaving the folded-snowflake on the table, she enclosed the mug in her chilly fingers. "Am I supposed to be disappointed?"

Devin said, "I'm a disappointment as a human being. I'm pretty sure no one ever thought, 'You know, vandalism and a budding alcohol problem? Great characteristics.'"

Marlie said, "I'm sure many people have thought, 'You know, facing the consequences of one's actions and turning everything around? Great characteristics.'" She sipped, and although it was a little too hot, the cocoa carried a faint aura of vanilla that blended perfectly with the creamy chocolate. "Also, it's not up to me to be disappointed in you. Your mother is proud."

Devin huffed. "My mother would be proud of anything I did."

"She's not proud of Rachel." Marlie glanced down. "My parents aren't proud of me, so trust me on this—you're doing fine. Anita's proud of you. I'm proud of you. Everyone goes off the road, sometimes, but not everyone pushes the car back out of the ditch and then drives straight afterward."

This time, Devin's silence didn't seem to be from exhaustion. He was looking at her, caught in a pause between one moment and the next.

Uncomfortable, Marlie sipped more of the hot chocolate. "This is good. Thank you."

Devin said, "Didn't you always think I was a troublemaker?"

Marlie looked over the rim of her mug. "You were the good kind of troublemaker, the kind who climbed out the window when you were bored."

Devin said, "To be fair, I only got bored because school was boring."

"We were all bored. You were the only one who figured out how to open the window wide enough to climb out." Marlie paused. "And you never admitted it, but when the holiday display table went on fire in the middle school hallway, that had your fingerprints all over it."

Devin raised his hands. "I didn't intend to set fire to anything. They had that pretty candle on it. I only lit the candle. It wasn't my fault there was a sign taped over it that caught fire and then dropped onto the table and ignited everything else."

Marlie giggled. "Flaming pine cones make such a nice snapping sound."

"So do fire extinguishers." Devin shrugged. "Fire alarms, less nice, but at least we got out of that math quiz. I count that as a total win."

Marlie said, "And, dare I mention it—?"

Devin folded his hands and made a solemn face. "The letter S."

Marlie raised her mug. "To the letter S."

"Look, it's not every day you find an entire roll of reflective letter stickers. They deserved to be stuck somewhere."

Making an earnest expression, Marlie leaned forward. "And it stands to reason, therefore, that you needed to figure out exactly where they should go."

"You're acting as though I didn't have help, although I will take the identities of my helpers right to the grave." He hesitated. "I notice you didn't say that had my fingerprints all over it."

"It most certainly did!" Marlie laughed. "There were reflective S stickers on everything, and we kept finding them for months. The narrow sides of the doors, any sign in the school with the misfortune to have an S on it, random windows, street signs, fence posts—"

"Five hundred stickers!" Devin exclaimed, looking both innocent and urgent. "Do you have any idea how hard it is to find places for five hundred stickers?"

"And yet, you succeeded!" Marlie laughed. "Going above and beyond, you worked tirelessly for months to stick one to every flat surface in Hartwell."

He reached for the folded-up triangle on the table. "I will always go above and beyond."

She said, "I expect nothing less," before realizing he was opening out the snowflake, and it was just a circle of hearts.

It flared open in his hands, and he looked from it to her, wide-eyed. He reached for the cut-out heart shapes that had fallen to the table and opened one of those as well.

Marlie's brain dial-toned. She couldn't even make a quip about hearts warm enough to melt snowflakes. In fact, she couldn't come up with any banter at all.

It turned out that was for the best because he leaned around the table and kissed her.

She responded before he could pull away, closing her eyes and resting her hand behind his neck. His wasn't the aroma of pine as much as chocolate and fry oil and soap, but the cocktail of scents was uniquely him.

Devin slipped off his chair and knelt in front of her, and she kissed him urgently, letting the feeling sweep through her. The man, the mischief-maker, the crush who'd nestled into the curves of her folded paper heart from the time she was a little girl carrying a pencil box and a hot lunch tray—this man was right here, right in front of her, his lips pressed to hers.

In high school, she'd have squealed at the thought of kissing this dark-eyed, dusky-voiced rascal, but now she managed nothing more than a sigh.

Jazz was right. Bri was right. He'd wanted to kiss her, and here he was.

Devin sat back on his heels, then breathed, "It was the stickers, wasn't it? I had no idea." When Marlie giggled, he took her hands. "This is going to be an amazing Christmas."

"Thanks to you." She kissed him again. "You've made it

an amazing Christmas for me."

———————✦———————

They moved to the couch, the TV playing a Boston Pops Christmas concert at a low volume so no one could hear them from the other rooms. Devin switched on the gas fireplace, then pulled a checkered throw blanket over them both. Marlie wrapped her arms around his waist.

"I'm ruining your evening." She rested her cheek against his shoulder. "You probably wanted to go downstairs and fall unconscious."

"I'll cope with the devastation." His tone changed to a more strained note. "Okay, so—you're sure you're okay with this?"

Marlie closed her eyes. "I may fall asleep on you, and you may not be okay with that."

"I'm kind of stunned, that's all. I'm not in your league." He tensed. "I mean, you're out of my league, not that I'm some kind of amazing catch."

She said, "Am I that touchy?"

He huffed. "It would be just like me to ruin things five minutes after they started."

The orchestra had begun playing "Sleigh Ride," and the instruments mimicked the gait of a horse and the ringing of sleigh bells. She'd never ridden in a sleigh. If you had to get around by sleigh, though, it would be an everyday thing, not just for Christmas. Would this song even have been considered festive to a farmer in 1700?

Devin's heart beat under her ear. It was just warm enough beneath the blanket, and while she watched the flickering flames, her breathing deepened.

"I was crushing on you," she murmured. "In high school."

"Really?" His arm tightened around her shoulders. "You never let on."

Not even once. Not just timidity had hidden it, but also the thought of her parents if she brought home a boy whose father was in prison, a boy whose name crowned the top ten list of regulars in detention, a boy who'd made headlines at age nine doing something breathtakingly dangerous and from which he emerged without a scratch.

He added, "Given who I was back then, it's probably better you waited."

She said, "We all needed to grow up."

He squeezed her. "You were an adult from the time you were seven."

Was that true? And if it was true, was that a good thing?

The song changed to "I'll Be Home for Christmas," something Marlie wasn't going to be. Her parents hadn't ever done Christmas at home, though. It was always a vacation somewhere, maybe her grandparents' houses, maybe a ski lodge in Vermont, maybe a trip to a warmer climate. They'd brought a few presents to open Christmas morning, but the real presents would be waiting for them at home.

At age fifteen, Marlie had spent Christmas morning in front of a fireplace like this one, the kind you turned on and off. She'd pulled the coffee table near the hearth so she could be warm while she folded origami cubes with the paper she'd gotten that morning. Dad was reading, and Mom was on the phone with her sister. Marlie had sat, creasing and folding, creating cube after cube and germinating an idea.

Halfway through, she took the sparkling green paper she'd set aside for special. This would be the only green cube she made, that way she'd be able to tell it apart. Without her father taking any notice, Marlie wrote in the center of the page with a gel pen, "I wish."

Then, quickly, she creased the page, folding and eyeballing the measurements to make sure this one cube was the most perfect of all the cubes. She finished off the edges of the cube just as her mother came into the living room and said, "For heaven's sake, Marlie, make something new. How many paper dice do you need?"

Marlie reached for her origami book, also new, and started folding something else. But there, in the corner of her vision, was that pile of cubes for her friends.

And one sparkly green cube.

For Devin.

Who now said he'd never opened it.

Because, sometimes, a mystery is best to remain unsolved, and a secret is best to keep.

I wish.

She started awake when Devin kissed her forehead. "You need to get to bed, sleepy."

The song had changed again, midway through "Santa Claus is Coming to Town." "I bet you say that to Cory, too."

"And then he fusses." He stood away from her to shut off the gas fireplace and the television, and she tucked the blanket around herself, still warm from his body heat. "But you deserve better than crashing on the couch, and we both have to get up in the morning."

Reluctantly, Marlie set the blanket aside, and then he kissed her again. The hallway was chilly, but he waited until she got into her room to turn out the lights and go downstairs.

I wish.

But sometimes, wishes come true.

CHAPTER TWELVE

Marlie awoke to the sounds of Cory and Anita getting breakfast. Bri and Jazz had already left the room.

She dropped back onto the pillow, staring at the line of sunlight across the ceiling. How many times had Devin kissed her last night? Were those kisses the bad judgment of two exhausted people under the spell of a holiday? When he'd held her hand beneath the blanket, his fingers intertwined with hers, had that been a dream?

To keep the dream forever, she'd have to stay under the blankets, listening to murmurs from the kitchen. Dreams dispersed when you got out of bed. Instead, she could remain in the liminal space between late night and early morning, the cozy nook between December 23rd and Christmas Eve. Nothing else had to inhabit that space, and nothing could shatter that peace and potential.

With a sigh, she snuggled down in the bed again, and she must have fallen asleep once more because she started when she heard sounds in the room.

"Sorry." That was Jazz's voice. "I didn't mean to wake you."

Marlie reached for her phone and checked the time. "Oh, wow. I slept in."

"No biggie. We're on vacation." Jazz sat on the edge of the air mattress. "Well? Did you and Devin stay up all night, coiling yourselves in Christmas lights?"

In a low voice, Marlie said, "There may or may not have been some kissing."

Although she kept her voice down, Jazz mock-squealed, and she bounced a bit. "I knew it!"

Marlie pulled her hoodie on over her red flannel pajamas. "I keep trying to decide if it really happened."

"You don't ordinarily hallucinate entire men." She beamed. "Well, get yourself out of bed because Devin is out there drinking coffee, and we're making plans for the day."

He smiled the instant she entered the kitchen, looking just as good this morning, if unshaven. "Merry Christmas Eve. How do you like your coffee?"

"Hot, and in a mug?" She tried to hide the compulsive grin.

He arched his eyebrows. "Milk...? Sugar...?"

The teasing continued through breakfast, with Devin looking simultaneously pleased and smug. Jazz had stars in her eyes the whole time, and she kept breaking off to text someone—possibly her husband—while Bri just seemed amused.

Cory, fortunately, had no idea what was going on, and was just so very, very, very, very (did she mention very?) excited for Christmas Eve. "And we're going to Uncle Devin's work because they're going to have a party." He seemed to have forgotten that everyone already knew this—

in fact, that everyone else had been the ones to tell him about it. Instead, for this morning, Cory could be the bringer of repeated tidings. "They'll have music and cake and cookies, and Santa Claus is going to be there, and you get to take your picture with him, and then you tell him what you want, and then he'll get it for you."

Jazz rested her chin on her clasped hands. "What are you wishing for?"

"A car!"

Although Anita choked on her coffee, Cory showcased an effusive grin as he bowled bravely forward. "If I have a car, I can go places! I can go to school, and then I can go drive to see my mom because my mom is far away so that's why I need a car because you can't walk that far."

Anita's eyebrows shot up, and her voice took on a warning note. "Cory, it's more than distance."

When the boy hesitated, Marlie could see right down the path this conversation was going to take—right to the realization that his mother didn't love him. He'd connect the dots that his mother had abandoned him and was never coming back, and the reason he couldn't see her wasn't that there wasn't a car or his grandmother didn't have time to drive him to see her. The reason was—she didn't care.

It was a terrible thing to realize, and he shouldn't realize it during the first real Christmas he'd ever had.

To head it off, Marlie said to Devin, "Well, he's definitely your nephew."

Devin tilted his head.

Marlie turned to Cory. "Do you know that when Uncle Devin was nine, he actually drove the family car?"

Anita tensed, but Jazz snorted. "I remember that. Didn't you make the national papers or something?"

Devin lowered his voice. "I really don't think this is a great line of conversation."

Cory said, "What happened? Where did he go?"

Marlie said, "Your uncle was smart. As in, the smartest boy in the class. He watched what everyone did, and later on, he could repeat it. So, while he was sitting in the car, he watched everything your grandmother did to drive. Then, one day in the summer, he wanted ice cream and there wasn't any ice cream...so he took the keys and took your mom and your aunt, and he drove them to get ice cream."

Cory's mouth opened. "Really?"

Marlie said, "He was only nine years old."

Devin put in, "I was eight. And Cory, it was a really dumb thing to do. I could have hurt my sisters. I could have wrecked the car."

Marlie said, "But he didn't. He was actually a better driver than some people who've had lessons and gotten tested to become drivers, because he made it six miles to the ice cream stand. And then he bought the ice creams. And then he drove home."

Leaning against the wall, Devin folded his arms. "You forgot to add, I bought one for mom, too, although the cops didn't let me bring it inside before it melted."

Cory started. "The cops?"

Marlie said, "Your uncle made it almost all the way back before a police officer saw a little boy driving a car that was way too big for him. When Uncle Devin parked the car in the driveway, the officer got out and told him he should never do that again."

"To really drive, you have to be sixteen years old. You have to take classes. You have to be tall enough to see over the dashboard, and your legs have to be long enough to push the brake pedal all the way down." He crouched across the table from Cory. "I'm serious. You can't do that. Grandma Anita got into a lot of trouble because of me. She didn't know I took her keys, but the police and a lot of social workers had to make sure Grandma wasn't being a bad mom."

Cory sounded affronted. "Grandma is a wonderful mom."

Marlie had never thought about the situation from the point of view of the adults. The kids at school, of course, had just been in awe that Devin had *driven a car*. Marlie had heard at least one teacher saying if they had to pick a third grader who'd steal a car and make a round trip perfectly the first time, hands down, it would have been Devin. They'd said it with pride and more than a little laughter. A radio show had picked up the story, and one of the DJs had quipped, "What a hero. I'd have done the same for ice cream." Devin had even buckled his sisters into their booster seats.

But ever after that, whenever Marlie had mentioned Devin in the presence of her parents, it had always been, "Oh, the little car thief?" When they'd graduated, her mother had said, "I see the car thief didn't drop out."

Devin said, "Little Man, listen to me. You can't ask Santa for a car. A car is a very big responsibility, and you're still a little guy. I'll teach you to drive when it's time. But until then, you have to be safe. That means you ride in your car seat, and you let me or Grandma take you places."

Cory frowned. "I can be safe."

"You can be safe in the back." He glanced at Marlie. "No matter what your uncle did, you can't go doing the same things."

Jazz said, "At the very least, you need to be able to read the traffic signs."

"I can do that." Cory beamed. "There's a traffic sign in Uncle Devin's room!"

Wide-eyed, Devin said, "Uh...you need to know how to read all of them."

Marlie cocked her head. "You have a traffic sign in your room?"

"And a big orange cone." Cory giggled. "It would make a big ice cream cone. You could fit in gallons."

Devin stood, shaking his head.

Marlie said, "Wait, I need to know. What traffic sign?"

Anita folded her arms. "Actually, I want to know that, too."

As if he wanted to sink into the floor, Devin offered, "Sometimes...these things just follow you home?"

Cory laughed as he reached for another donut hole. "It's so funny."

Anita said, "It better not be one of the signs that has a GPS tracker on the back."

"Nothing so serious." Devin rolled his eyes. "All right, fine."

Carrying her coffee, Marlie followed Devin downstairs, trailed by Jazz and Bri, while Cory pushed past them. Anita came, too. "I need to know if the Department of Public Works is about to bang on the front door."

"It's been years. You never go into my room, and you weren't around when I moved in." He paused at the door, then looked Marlie in the eye. "Remember what I was telling you about being something of a troublemaker?"

Marlie said, "I had no idea."

He opened the door and flipped on the lights.

Devin's "room" was more like a suite, was Marlie's first impression. Although it was one large open space, he'd used the furniture to divide it into sections. A tall dresser and a portable closet segmented off the bed from the rest of the room. As promised, an orange traffic cone sat atop the dresser.

Marlie murmured, "What danger is it warning you away from?"

Devin said, "If anyone's driving down here in the first place, I'd think the danger should be obvious."

He had a gaming computer, of course, and there, on the wall opposite the monitor, right where the webcam would capture it on every video call, was a reflective orange sign reading, "Unpaved Trenches Ahead."

Behind Marlie, Anita murmured, "Oh for crying out loud..."

Jazz was laughing. Marlie said, "Where did you even get that?"

"More importantly," Bri said, "the day after you got it, were half a dozen cars lining the bottom of an unpaved trench?"

"The trench had been paved over for a week and a half. I thought it was funny. As in, obviously you shouldn't careen into an unpaved trench." Devin's nose wrinkled. "For that matter, aren't most trenches by definition unpaved? Anyhow, they'd been paved. The sign was a lie. I decided to give it a good home."

Marlie crossed the room toward it. "I admire your dedication to cleaning up the streets of Hartwell."

Cory slammed into her thigh, saying, "Give me the cone."

Devin said, "He wants to wear it as a hat."

As Marlie reached for it, he added, "That wasn't

permission for him to wear it as a hat."

Looking down, Marlie said to Cory, "You'd look like an orange elf. Does Santa give presents to orange elves?"

Cory frowned. "Doesn't Santa give presents to everyone?"

"The elves work for him already, so I'm not sure." Marlie scooped him up onto her hip, and he reached out to touch the sign, too. "Maybe they don't want presents because they've been working so hard to make presents for everyone else."

"I thought everyone got presents." He reached out in her arms, nearly squirming away. "I want that cone."

Devin grabbed him before he fell and stood him back on his feet. "No cones. No signs." He gestured toward the door. "And no—really, I mean no—cars."

CHAPTER THIRTEEN

Pine garlands coiled around the cast iron gateway at the main entrance of Hartwell's town park. Just inside was the Christmas Village.

Memories crashed into Marlie. Her parents had taken her here. So had her grandparents. It was a Hartwell tradition. There had been a school trip, too.

Devin had climbed a tree during that trip, hadn't he? First off the bus, right up the nearest tree, and then basically having his own self-guided tour afterward. She'd seen him go up and said nothing, but when it was time to come home, she'd made sure he'd made it back onto the bus.

He had. Pink cheeked and bright-eyed, he'd sat in the front row, eating a steamy pretzel he'd gotten from a vendor.

The vendors were back again this year. Maybe she and Devin could split a hot pretzel.

At Marlie's side, Cory gasped, "Grandma, look," then put

his hand up and clutched Marlie's. He started dragging her toward the exhibits while she glanced at Anita, helpless. Cory clearly thought he had a different adult. Anita was snickering, though, so Marlie let it happen.

Devin appeared by her side. "Someone's about to learn the danger of identifying adults based on their jeans.

Cory kept yanking her arm to drag her forward until they were in front of the first exhibit. Each station was set up in a wooden shelter with plexiglass on three sides, and inside were miniatures, lights, and moving figures. The first was Santa's workshop, complete with tiny elves hammering in rhythm, a train laden with toys as it chugged around the workshop, and Santa at a desk in the back, reading a long list.

Cory looked up, then started when he saw Marlie.

Devin picked him up. "Little Man, you grabbed the wrong hand. Here." He leaned forward so Cory could get a better view. "What do you think?"

The exhibit was playing music, difficult to hear but also slightly out of tune. Some parts of the exhibit seemed worn, and Marlie wondered how many more years these exhibits would last.

Cory breathed, "They're so cool."

Marlie said, "The pieces were all hand-made by one man. He used to have a machine shop, and if he didn't have anything to do, he'd work on carving these miniatures."

Cory beamed. "Let's see another."

Devin carried him through the crowd. At the next exhibit, though, looking at an assortment of reindeer in stalls while an elf polished a harness, he set Cory down and took Marlie's hand.

Her breath frothed up in the chill, but inside, she

warmed all over. The air smelled sharp, and the sky was brilliant. The crowd was a constant murmur, punctuated by Cory's excited narration of everything he could identify. Bri and Jazz and Anita were still admiring the first display. This was Devin and Marlie's moment, shared alone in the midst of so many others.

Each display had its own marvels and its own music. A living room on Christmas morning with a family opening their presents before a tiny decorated tree, and a miniature fireplace with an animated flame. A nativity scene with farm animals and a delicate manger filled with individual shavings of wood to represent straw. Forest animals exchanging nuts and berries. Cory kept explaining everything they were looking at as though only he could see it, and in his stream of talk, Marlie re-experienced what Christmas was to someone who'd never enjoyed it before. Also, at every exhibit, Devin kept his hand around hers, his body close to hers, and in doing so, drew her heart closer to his.

Marlie had no idea Christmas could be like this. If she'd ever felt it this way, she'd forgotten.

At the end there was a playground with a life-size sleigh and reindeer, and Cory ran to hang on the reindeers' necks and climb into the sleigh.

Marlie was still watching him when Devin said, "Don't do that again—telling Cory about the dangerous stuff I did."

Marlie tensed. "What? Why?"

"Because I don't want him to do it, too. Couldn't you see the wheels turning in his head when you told him I figured out how to drive a car—and then drove it to get ice cream? This is a kid who's already asked for a car." Devin scowled, but not at her. He was just scowling off into the distance. It made his eyes darker and his face sharper. "You haven't been with him long enough to see it, but he was figuring out how he could get our car keys and do the same thing."

Marlie stepped back. "I'm sorry. I didn't realize."

"He's wicked smart, and he's charming, but he's also a free spirit. Rachel must have been awful to him. He came here like this mix of a baby and a little adult. He knew how to make himself food, but first he would ask if we wanted him to make something for us. He would unlock the front door and get the mail at age three, and he'd try to console my mother when she looked sad, but he didn't know how to ask for help tying his shoes. Anger is terrifying to him." He shook his head. "The therapist said that's because of neglect, that Rachel blew hot and cold, so he learned to survive by parenting her."

Marlie shivered, but not from the weather. She took Devin's hand. He didn't squeeze her fingers.

He still stared away from her. Cory raced around the playground, trailing other kids who thought he was just too much fun not to play with. Devin had been like that, too. "You didn't know any of that, but the point is, he doesn't understand that he's a child. He thinks he can be a little adult because that's what Rachel demanded."

Marlie swallowed hard. "I'm sorry."

"My probation officer wouldn't want me to say out loud the things I want to happen to Rachel." He huffed. "At least Cory has a good family now, and we'll provide for him. We're letting him be a kid. But he's got some of the same genes that made me a hell-raiser, and, well..." Devin snorted. "I'd prefer not to encourage that."

Marlie ventured, "Or you'll get some of the same calls

from the school that your mom got?"

He laughed. "I have no idea how my mother kept a straight face. They told her once, 'Devin was engaging in an unexpected behavior,' which I guess they were using instead of saying I'd been an out and out hellion. After she heard what I'd done, she told them, 'That's not unexpected at all. Why didn't you expect it? As soon as you started telling the story, I expected it.'"

Marlie covered her mouth with her hands. "Oh, no."

"Good training for when I have to keep up with him." He shook his head. "Anyhow, as long as we're here, since you're something of a magpie, let's look at the lights."

The town had wound light strings up into arches over the path circling the pond, and even in the full daylight, their sparkle glittered like magic.

"This must be gorgeous at night," Marlie said as they walked.

Devin nodded. "I came here once after work, to unkey. They turn the lights off at midnight, but until then, it's silent and brilliant. When no one else is here, everything feels so stark."

It being Christmas Eve, silence and starkness weren't in the cards. People were walking and talking, jostling and weaving around clusters of other people. Everyone had preparations to get back to—wrapping or cooking or cleaning.

"I'd have liked to see that," Marlie murmured.

"I didn't think to take you last night." Devin shrugged. "We seemed to be doing okay anyhow."

"Last night was just fine." She beamed up at him. "How far do the lights go?"

He walked with her, gesturing toward the pond. "The

path wraps all the way round, I'd guess about a half mile? Maybe a little less. There's a bit of a hill over there where it disappears into the trees, and I think that's the point where you're in the dark."

Marlie glanced back at Cory. "He's having a good time at the playground."

"Yeah, and drawing quite an entourage. I don't want to just leave him, although I guarantee he wouldn't notice." Devin chuckled. "On the other hand," and he led her off to the side of the path, "if I were to kiss you under these trees before I head in to work, he wouldn't notice that, either."

Then Devin did, taking her into his arms with a sweetness that sent away all thoughts of weather and cars and sad stories. The crowd disappeared for a moment, and Marlie wished that moment could last all morning.

Instead, it ended. Devin wrapped his own scarf around Marlie's neck, tucking it under itself. "Here, you need this." He kissed her forehead. "Stay and enjoy the lights, but while you're doing that, I want you to remember how much you light up my world."

CHAPTER FOURTEEN

The Willowgate Assisted Living Community Christmas party was a lot more festive than Marlie had feared. Despite how Devin had described the place, she'd defaulted to her memories of her great aunt in a sterile building devoid of personality, and also devoid of happiness.

Willowgate, by contrast, squatted at the center of fifty acres of manicured landscape, ribboned with walking paths, clusters of pines, and benches. It even had a pond. The facility wasn't one structure as much as a collection of white-sided buildings joined by covered passages. Indoors was all warmth and carpeting and plants. "Welcome!" exclaimed the security guard, dressed as Mrs. Claus, and with that, Cory was in heaven. They signed in, everyone on the guest list as Devin had promised, and after leaving their coats in an adjacent room, they went to the dining room.

Jazz exclaimed, "This is so nice," and Marlie realized then that she'd scanned the whole room searching only for

Devin without seeing anything else.

A twelve-foot tree dominated the event, strung with white lights and baubled to within an ounce of collapse. On the far wall was a buffet station, all the serving trays still closed. Dozens of round tables stood with tiny Christmas tree centerpieces, and at the far end of the room stood a red throne where, presumably, Santa would hold court.

An elf, whose nametag identified her as a CNA, handed them pamphlets. "There's a video game room down the hall," she said in what sounded like a well-practiced speech, "plus a TV room, a quiet lounge at the end of the Western wing, a music room with a piano on the Eastern wing, and we'll be bringing out an ice cream bar at the end of the evening in the meeting room by the front entrance."

Music began, and Marlie turned to find an oompah band in the corner. Cory giggled. "That's a big trumpet!"

"It's a tuba," Anita said. "Do you recognize the other instruments?"

She took him by the hand, and Marlie glanced around again for Devin.

Bri said, "Let's stake out a table."

Working tonight, Devin wouldn't be able to eat with them. His team had set up a nice party for the residents and their families, though. Marlie headed to one of the snack stations for cheese and crackers, sliced sausages, and a crostini.

Had Devin been the one slicing these? Had he been hard at work for two hours, wondering which piece of cheese would be Marlie's, and whether she'd know he was thinking of her when he sliced it?

She sighed as she looked out the window. It would be dark by four o'clock, the perfect time to revisit the lights on the path, but Devin wouldn't be free until well after ten. It was already freezing outside. His scarf was still tucked up in her jacket sleeve.

The party had activity tables, so Marlie found the one where Cory was coloring a Christmas tree. "I want an accordion," he said. "If Santa won't give me a car, then maybe Santa will give me an accordion."

Anita said, "And Santa can bring me some ibuprofen."

Marlie said, "Maybe a Honda Accordion?"

Anita's mouth twitched. "And industrial ear protection."

The stacks of coloring pages were separated by one colorful slice of paper every hundred sheets or so. Marlie flipped through and realized they actually divided into groups of different coloring pages, so she separated the stacks to make all the options visible. Then she took one of the blank pink pages and started folding a paper crane.

Although the room was noisy, folding paper was always personal, always quiet. Marlie knew what her fingertips should sound like as they slid across the folds, and what the paper would sound like as the crease took form. She could recreate those in her mind as Cory pressed deep into his paper with a green crayon, and she could focus on the tiny world she was creating, the little creature taking form beneath her hands.

Origami had a peace all its own, the challenge of a single sheet of paper folding around itself until it became something with multiple twists and bends and eventually a new identity.

One of the residents joined them to color beside Cory. When she saw Marlie folding a paper crane, though, she wanted to watch. Then she wanted Marlie to make another paper crane to teach her the entire process, and by the time

Marlie had finished the second paper crane, two more residents had taken seats.

Marlie laughed. "Isn't this the children's activity table?"

"We're all children in this world," said a white-haired woman with bright eyes. "What else can you make?"

Cory exclaimed, "Snowflakes!"

"Then you need to make us some," said the bright-eyed woman, handing Marlie another sheet of paper.

"I'd need scissors," she said, except a moment later, someone had procured scissors, so now Marlie was creasing the letter-sized paper and cutting to make a square, then folding the triangle shape. She said to Cory, "What kind of shape should I make?"

"A pretty star like you made for the tree," Cory said, which could have been any of a dozen stars, so Marlie went for a typical snowflake shape with narrow spines and rays off the edges.

Jazz stopped by the table. "Oh, for Pete's sake, Marlie, you are *such* a showoff."

Marlie exclaimed, "They asked me!"

"Yeah, I'm sure, they were walking around the room, asking every single person, 'Hey, do you know how to do origami snowflakes?' and when they got to you, finally—finally!—they found someone who could."

Bri chucked Jazz on the shoulder. "Leave Marlie alone."

"Yes, leave her alone." The bright-eyed woman shook her head. "Wait, Marlie? Marlie Bancroft?"

When Marlie started, the woman added, "I'm Mrs. Addison, your second grade teacher."

"Oh my gosh!" Jazz laughed. "Oh, then you totally knew Marlie could make cranes and snowflakes. You didn't even need to ask."

Mrs. Addison arched her eyebrows. "But I didn't know it was Marlie."

Cory said, "Make another snowflake," but Marlie shook her head, mouthing, *Not yet.*

The other two women wanted to know how she was and why she was in Hartwell and whether her parents were here as well. Marlie tried to laugh it off with, "They're on a boat somewhere warm where the sun hasn't set," and that neatly deflected the conversation toward Anita as the women talked about how generous she was to open her home to these three nice young ladies for Christmas.

Cory huffed. "Miss Marlie, make another snowflake."

Mrs. Addison said, "Oh, sorry, go ahead and do that for him."

While folding the starting triangle, Marlie said to Cory, "What should I make next?"

"One like you made Uncle Devin," he said, "with the heart shapes all over it."

Marlie's actual heart skipped a beat.

First off, Cory hadn't even been in the kitchen when she'd made it for him. Had he? He'd been asleep the whole time, or so she'd thought.

Secondly, why were all the white-haired ladies suddenly staring at Marlie as if she'd belched?

Ignoring everyone's expressions, Marlie traced half-heart edges on the triangle, but she knew how they'd be looking at her. There would be disgust and outrage and pity. They'd be thinking about Devin's past and her past, and how someone whose own family abandoned her would never be able to get anyone better than a childhood car thief who'd slashed a creepy man's tires while three sheets to the wind.

Her eyes stung, and she needed to cut the paper, but her hands weren't steady.

Working with the snowflake, it felt as if the whole world went silent again, but this time, it was an accusatory silence. It was the same silence of her mother knowing Marlie wasn't good enough to afford a destination wedding at Christmas. It was the silence of never measuring up to her brother and being cast off because she'd never be the good sibling. And now here was Mrs. Addison, who'd conferenced with her parents and who'd also had her brother in class, knowing everything, judging everything. Judging Devin. Judging her.

Marlie wasn't good enough.

As she cut the paper, folded bits dropped to the table, tiny folded hearts with creases down the center. It was appropriate enough. When she unfolded the snowflake, there were six empty heart-shaped spaces.

From behind her, she heard Devin's voice. "How's everyone doing?"

Marlie cringed. Cory exclaimed, "Miss Marlie is making snowflake hearts, and this lady used to be her teacher."

Devin said, "My teacher, too."

Cory gasped, "Really?"

Marlie didn't want to look at him, but Jazz was saying, "Cory told us you asked Marlie to make you a heart-shaped snowflake."

"That's not what he did!" Marlie exclaimed, looked right at Jazz. She sounded panicked, and she was speaking too quickly. "Cory wasn't even there when I made it."

Mrs. Addison said to Devin, "But even so, I think she'd be good for you."

Marlie's ears were ringing so hard that she nearly didn't

hear Devin quip, "Thank you for the endorsement. I'll be sure to consult you about all my life decisions," at which Mrs. Addison laughed, but then another voice cut through.

"I don't think so, at all!" The woman across the table glared at Devin. "Does she know about you?"

Mrs. Addison exclaimed, "Shirley!"

"Does she?" Shirley glared at Marlie. "Do you know he's here as a prison work release?"

Devin said, "I never went to prison in the first place, so, no, she doesn't know that because it's not true."

The woman huffed.

Cory said, "Uncle Devin, Miss Marlie made you more hearts."

It was too much, too many people, too many assumptions. Shirley—did Marlie even know Shirley?—was glaring at Devin as though he were a felon and Marlie as though she were selling herself cheap. Mrs. Addison clearly thought Marlie was dating downward. And Cory wore a brilliant obliviousness to everything except how awesome it was that Miss Marlie could cut paper shapes that turned wood pulp into hearts.

That look on Shirley's face was going to be the same look on Mom's face, and Dad's face, and then next year, when her family flew to Singapore for some random third cousin's graduation, Marlie wouldn't be flying to that, either. "She's dating a felon, so she can't leave the country," Mom would say. "He's a car thief or something," and it was one more nail in the coffin.

Resting a hand on Marlie's shoulder, Devin leaned over her to take the paper heart cutouts. Marlie tensed beneath his touch. "Thank you, Cory. Did Miss Marlie make these as a Christmas present?"

Cory's voice got solemn. "She made them because I asked."

"That's a good reason to do things." Devin looked down at Marlie, hand still on her shoulder, and he slid it closer to her neck. "Is he right? Did you only make them because he asked?"

Devin's touch wasn't warming her. Instead, it created chills. Her throat was tight, but she managed to say, "I would never call Cory a liar."

It was close enough to banter that it should have passed muster, but Devin realized then how tense she was—or how scared of being touched. He made the connection in a heartbeat and withdrew.

That didn't return warmth to her. If anything, it left her colder.

Devin returned his attention to the ladies. "Have you tried the snack tables? Mrs. Watson, we made sure to put out your favorite chips, and I used your onion dip recipe. They're going fast. You should get some before they're gone."

His voice was measured enough that Marlie wondered if Shirley Watson had an instant-read digital thermometer in her reticule and would be sticking it into the dip to make sure he'd served it at the appropriate chill.

Afterward, maybe she'd jab the thing into Marlie's heart to make sure it wasn't getting too warm.

Sitting in Anita's living room with Jazz and Bri, this had seemed so simple. Cuddling with Devin, it had seemed even more simple. Anonymous in a crowd? Simple.

Here under the lights and the scrutiny, it wasn't simple at all. People knew him, and they knew her. They were disappointed in Devin, and they'd already known she was a disappointment to her family.

Devin said, "I need to get back to the kitchen. I just wanted to check up on everyone." He gestured a wave to the entire table. "Enjoy the party."

Was he being cold? Was Jazz staring at them both as though she'd seen every one of Marlie's innermost thoughts?

Marlie took another pink paper and began folding. Folding was easy. Folding married the dull side of the paper against itself so people could see only the shiny outside. Folding and cutting was even easier because people saw what was left behind and not the parts that went away.

Paper snowflakes were easiest of all. Fold until everything is hidden. Trace half the shape people want to see, and shade out the stuff they don't want. Cut away all the shaded spots and pretend they never existed, and people will be able to enjoy what they wanted to be there in the first place. It was, in the end, strategic mutilation.

She could love Devin. She'd loved him as a child and loved him as a teen, and she could love him as an adult. Now, though, she knew the minute she did that, no one else would ever again love her. If that happened, how could she love herself?

CHAPTER FIFTEEN

It wasn't so much that Devin avoided them as that he just wasn't around.

He was busy. Marlie could explain it that way, but to her it seemed he went out of his way to avoid her—which meant avoiding his mother. Chasing Cory, Anita didn't notice. Bri had excused herself to the music room to play Christmas songs on the piano, and Jazz was in one of the smaller conference rooms, trying to get her husband on the phone.

That left Anita, Cory, and Marlie together while Cory devoured a pre-dinner cupcake topped with two inches of frosting.

"They make the atmosphere nice, here," Anita said. "I'm glad Devin got the job. He has a lot of latitude in the kitchen to run things the way he wants, and they give him enough interesting work that he doesn't get bored."

Marlie swallowed hard. "Half the things he did as a kid, I think he did them because he got bored."

Anita shook her head. "There's only so much you can do to keep a kid like him occupied. I'd ask the teachers to give him extra work just to stop him from learning to pick locks or how to concoct a bomb from the ingredients in a school lunch, but he was always one step ahead. Here, being one step ahead is a good thing."

It was pitch black outside already, and not even dinner time.

Anita said, "Have you heard from your parents?"

"The wedding is tonight, so they're probably doing all sorts of things on the ship." She'd texted them pictures from the exhibit, of course, but they hadn't replied. For all Marlie knew, the ship could have gone down in an ocean vortex, breaking in half like the Titanic as the funnel pulled it under, and as the water lapped over the deck, her mother would have been saying, "Devin? Marlie wants to date the car thief?"

Marlie said, "I'm sorry I told Cory about the ice cream thing."

Cory looked up. Anita said, "Well, it's done." She noticed then how he looked studious. "You know a car is an adult responsibility now."

Cory nodded. "Then I need a bicycle."

Marlie said, "You could hold out for one of those self-driving cars. By the time you're old enough to drive, I bet they'll have those. You'll get in and tell it, 'Take me to school,' and it'll drive you there."

Cory didn't laugh the way she expected. Instead, he said, "Could I send the car to the grocery store, and it would pick up ice cream for me?"

Marlie paused. "Much better than driving there yourself."

"Yeah." He thought a moment. Then, "How would your car know how to find you?"

Before Marlie could answer, the lights flickered, and then over the loudspeaker came a distinctive, "Ho ho ho!"

Cory's eyes lit up. "Santa!"

Anita scrambled after him as he shot out of his chair toward the red throne in the corner. Marlie followed to where all the children thronged before a dais cordoned off by stanchions and ropes.

Accompanied by a troop of elves, Santa paraded into the room, handing out small candy canes while repeatedly ho-ho-ho-ing at everyone. He hammed it up, prompting the kids to do their own ho-ho-hos and following up with the inevitable, "I can't hear you!" so the kids yelled it louder.

How many of the residents had surreptitiously turned off their hearing aids?

The adults herded the kids into some semblance of a line, and Santa started inviting them up onto the dais one at a time to ask them what they wanted for Christmas. "And have you been a good little girl who will get lots of presents?" he asked the first, who nodded excitedly and asked for a name-brand doll with a name-brand outfit, much to the relief of her parent who was taking the photo. Then came the next kid, who after affirming an entire year full of excellent behavior that deserved lots of presents, asked for a farm playset and a painting kit.

Devin joined them. "Oh, good. I didn't miss him."

Anita said, "I'm going to get a picture, but if you can take video, that would be terrific. I'll send it to Rachel if she asks."

Devin's eyes darkened, but he didn't reply.

Cory turned toward Anita with wide eyes. He was second

in line, and Anita stepped around the barricade to ask what was wrong.

Marlie moved closer to Devin, who said, "You probably don't want to do that."

She tensed.

He huffed. "Look, you can fool them, but how long have I known you? When they introduced me for who I am, you were embarrassed. That's fine. But don't lead me on."

Marlie swallowed. "I wasn't leading you on."

"I feel led-on." The next kid went to Santa, and now Cory was next in line. Devin huffed. "You knew exactly who I was. I thought I knew exactly who you were, especially when you confided things I didn't already know. I can read the room, though. You crushed on me in high school, and then when you found out the things I did as an adult, you couldn't deal. Again, that's your right. But I'm not going to participate in the charade because each of us deserves someone who's willing to love everything about the other one, even their past."

Marlie said, "That's not it at all."

Devin said, "In the alcohol program, one of the things they said was we're more than the sum of our mistakes. I took that to heart. It's a shame you can't see it."

Marlie tried to grab his arm, but he sidled free and went to the front as Cory got invited onto the dais.

Cory stood before Santa, for the first time unnerved. Marlie had expected Cory to be excited, especially after the way he'd pushed to the front of the line. But now, before the man towering on the throne, big with his red coat and fur hat and long beard, Cory had become small and tremulous. Anita urged him to step closer, and Cory did, then stopped.

Santa leaned forward to talk to him. Marlie could see he'd instinctively changed his tone and posture to set Cory at ease, but Cory didn't unkey.

Meanwhile, Devin stood, ramrod straight like a soldier, videoing the whole thing. He wasn't going to look at Marlie again—not now, and not afterward. He'd said everything he needed to say, and while he'd gotten the whole thing backward, his decision seemed final enough that explaining wouldn't help. He'd get his wish, and her mother would unknowingly get hers.

After a minute, Cory stepped toward Santa and spoke in a soft voice. Santa frowned as he strained to catch the words. Had Cory asked for a car after all, or had he remembered his newfound love for the accordion? Or was there some other, extra thing he'd devised in the last hour?

Santa spent more time with Cory than he had with the previous kids, although maybe time was telescoping for Marlie.

She'd need to apologize to Devin. Afterward, she'd need to stay out of his way and not ruin his holiday. Fortunately, he was working again tomorrow because every person in this facility needed to eat, so she wouldn't have to stay out of his way very long.

Santa handed Cory a goodie bag, but Cory didn't peek into it. Cory and Santa turned to the camera and smiled, Cory still seeming uneasy. Anita took more pictures, and then she brought Cory down from the dais so the next kid could bound up.

Coming up alongside Marlie, Jazz said, "He didn't look happy."

Bri was there, too. "My brothers used to wail whenever we got our pictures taken with Santa at the mall, although

I'd lay decent odds it was also because we'd waited in line for an hour, and everyone was hot and hungry."

Jazz snickered. "Speaking of hungry, when do they open up the food?"

Marlie said, "Devin's heading back to the kitchen, so— soon?"

Jazz teased, "And things are going well...?"

Rather than ruin their nights, too, she said, "Hey, did you get Ron on the phone?"

"He texted that we can talk later." Jazz sighed "I really do need to be the one working around his schedule, which I wouldn't mind except I don't know his schedule, and for obvious reasons, he can't always tell it to me."

Bri said, "The piano room is pretty neat, if you want to go in there later. I can teach Cory something simple."

Anita rejoined them with Cory on her hip. "Devin said after the kids are all done seeing Santa, they're going to open the buffet, and I want Cory to eat something that isn't sugar."

Marlie said to him, "What did you ask Santa for, Little Man?"

He said, "I asked for a car. He said that was too big to put under the tree, so I should ask for something else."

Marlie caught herself before saying, "Well, you knew you couldn't get a car," and instead what came out was, "I'm sorry."

Puzzled, Cory looked up at her, and she wondered then how often adults said that to kids, merely an acknowledgment of their disappointment without an attempt to solve it. *I'm sorry you can't have a car. I'm sorry your family got blown apart. I'm sorry that even with an awesome grandmother and uncle, you still miss your mother, and I'm sorry she doesn't deserve it.*

Cory hadn't been socialized enough yet to say, "That's okay." He just went with Anita back to their table.

The food was terrific. Marlie no longer wondered if Devin thought about feeding her when he'd cooked this stuff. In fact, if he did think about it, he probably thought now that it was just wasted time. Still, the spread was amazing. Stuffed shells, roasted seasoned chicken thighs, Swedish meatballs, rice pilaf, string beans with almonds, salad, taquitos, and pasta primavera. Cory ate twice his weight in entrees. Also sitting at their table were two residents and their respective children, so Marlie let them handle the talking.

Devin thought she was ashamed of his past. She'd need to set him straight about that somehow. If she could guarantee he'd read it, she could write a letter and get it all out without interruption. It made sense he'd think she believed she was degrading herself by being with him, but the real problem was how many people were out there judging. Judging everything. Talking behind your back. Glancing at each other when they thought you couldn't see. In the end, they'd know every setback in your life was of your own doing because when it came right down to it, you'd never been good enough.

Good enough meant having a job that could get you on a cruise on Christmas Eve to see your mother's roommate's daughter get married in the middle of the ocean. It meant having a career your parents could brag about and a house the size of Bangor and a designer puppy and a designer car and a designer spouse, and that was the moment you mattered. Up until then, you were like a tomato still green on the stalk, and they were all waiting for you to finish the job of becoming respectable.

The live music resumed, this time a "big band" rather than the oompah band. Cory wanted to see them, so Anita took him to the far corner.

Marlie sat in silence. Jazz looked out the window. "How is it only six o'clock?"

The day felt so long, what with a relationship both starting and ending in under twenty-four hours. How many extremes could a heart endure?

One of the other people at the table said to Marlie, "Are you the one who made those paper cranes before? Can you show me how?"

Cory and Anita returned, and Anita offered to help Cory make a paper crane of his own. As she demonstrated the crane-making steps, Marlie repeated the poem about the paper crane protecting children.

Cory said, "Does a paper crane protect grown ups, too?"

Marlie said, "I think so."

Cory nodded. "I want to make a lot."

Christmas cranes soon dotted the table, and Cory showed off the blue crane he'd made. "The others are white," he said, "but I can get crayons and color them."

He sprinted across the room, dodging around diners carrying plates, and returned with a handful of crayons. He sat next to one of the elderly gentlemen, and they colored together.

"They're getting ready to bring out dessert." Anita shook her head. "Just what Cory needs: additional sugar."

Cory pressed a pink crayon into Marlie's hand and told her to color one of the cranes. "I've never colored my cranes before," she said, and got to work on a wing. "Usually, the paper has the color already."

Cory said, "Sometimes you write inside the crane."

I wish.

Marlie said, "We didn't write inside any of these, did we?"

Cory just kept coloring until all the cranes lay covered in waxy residue, blue and pink and orange and purple. The older gentleman across the table said, "Shouldn't Christmas Cranes be red and green?"

Then dessert arrived, so Cory started shoving cranes into the goody bag he'd gotten from Santa. "Be careful not to crush them," said the man, "otherwise they won't be able to protect you."

Being more deliberate, Cory picked every single crane off the table, even the ones made by the older residents. "It's all right," the man assured Anita. "He had such a good time making them, and we want the paper cranes to protect this child."

The dessert hour began. Marlie browsed the pastries, which looked to have been brought in from outside rather than baked in-house. There were a dozen varieties of cookies, cream puffs, cannoli, and pistachio macaroons. In addition, Devin was slicing up and plating a sheet cake for anyone who went through the line. Marlie demurred that she was full, so she returned to the table. Jazz disappeared again to get Ron on the phone.

With her eyes closed, Marlie wondered how to handle a tense morning opening presents with Cory, a silent Christmas breakfast, and an early Christmas dinner. With any luck, she could find a way to avoid Devin. It might be best to fake a headache so at least he could open presents without broiling with anger the whole time.

Anita returned with a plate. "Didn't Cory come back to

you?"

Marlie started. "I thought he was with you."

"I sent him to the table with his cookies." She huffed. "He probably went back to fill his pockets."

"He might be with Bri or Jazz." Marlie stood. "I'll ask."

She passed by the craft tables, but he wasn't there. Santa wasn't seeing kids any longer, so no Cory there. Jazz was texting in a closed room, alone. Bri was in the music room, again without Cory.

Marlie said, "Cory's missing."

Bri stood. "Awesome. Five hundred people here, and we're looking for someone who's smaller than waist-high."

They returned to the dining room, only to find Anita still looking. Now she seemed concerned. "I have no idea where he went."

Bri said, "I'll check the game room," and Marlie said, "I'll go look in in the bathrooms. He can't have gone far."

At the restroom door, Marlie knocked, then opened the door and called, "Cory, are you in there?" Nothing. She checked the other bathrooms on the floor, but again, nothing.

By the time she got back to the dining room, Anita was talking rapidly with Devin, who looked by combinations angry and worried. She spun toward Marlie. "Not there?" When Marlie shook her head, Anita exclaimed, "His coat."

Marlie sprinted after her. "Why would he take his coat? Where would he be going?"

Behind them, Devin said, "Remember what I told you about him and car keys?"

Marlie said, "I'm sorry! I had no idea—"

"I actually don't care about you being sorry. I want to find him." Devin overshot the coat room and went right to the door guard. The current guard was dressed as an elf. "I'm looking for a four-year-old boy. Have you been here for the last half hour?"

The elf huffed. "Yeah, and I wouldn't let a little kid out of here alone."

Anita said to Marlie, "All the other entrances are alarmed because of the memory care patients. This is the only way he could get out of the building, so if he hasn't come here, he has to be inside."

Bri said, "Then I'm going back to the dining room. He's probably looking for scissors to cut snowflakes."

Anita said, "I can't imagine where he went, unless he wandered off with someone."

Devin poked at his phone and showed the elf a photo. "This kid. If you see him, keep him here and call me."

The elf started. "Wait, him?"

Marlie's heart sputtered to a stop.

The elf said, "He was with a family. They left ten minutes ago."

Chapter Sixteen

Devin yelled, but not much, because they needed to catch Cory.

Cory didn't have his coat. The elf had noticed him specifically because out of all the kids, Cory didn't have a coat on—but sometimes kids just get stubborn, so he'd figured that like most parents, these were picking their battles. Cory had trailed out after the group—several adults and three other kids, all of whom also had plastic bags from Santa and excited voices. Cory alone hadn't been speaking, and when the elf had said, "Good night, everyone," Cory had tightened his grip on his bag and rushed out the door.

Devin said, "And you didn't stop him?"

"I wasn't going to ask for his birth certificate!" the elf shot back. "It looked like one family!"

"Never mind." Anita went to the door. "I'm going after him. He may be in the parking lot."

"Stop." Devin turned to the elf. "You, call security. Get

someone to look at the parking lot footage so we can see if he went off with whoever that was."

The elf said, "And then I'll call the family because they signed out, and I know who they are. I'll ask if they know anything."

While the elf spoke into his walkie-talkie, Devin said to his mother, "You need your coat. Just because he's going to be freezing doesn't mean we need to be stupid. Go get that."

While Anita ran to the coatroom, Marlie texted Bri and Jazz to meet them at the front door—now.

Devin said to the elf, "Open the door. I'll check that our cars are still here."

Marlie said, "But your jacket—"

As the door clunked to unlock, Devin dashed outside. "Bring it to me. Always check the most dangerous place first."

Marlie ran to the coat room and grabbed her jacket from Anita, then grabbed Devin's as well. She still had his scarf stuffed into her sleeve, so she wrapped it around her neck, then pulled on her hat. From the speakers, a voice was calling a code that probably meant someone had eloped from the facility "Meet me and Devin in the parking lot," Marlie said, and tore off out the front entrance.

The air was brittle. Across the parking lot, she could hear Devin calling, "Cory!" but Marlie ran in the other direction, toward Anita's car. Up one row, across the back—and there, there was Anita's car. Unmoved. Cold. Locked.

Marlie pulled out her phone and with freezing fingers, texted Devin. "Not at your mom's car."

She pivoted and sprinted up the next aisle toward where Jazz had parked. Would Cory have stolen Jazz's keys?

Except no, again, the car was cold and dark. Undisturbed.

"Cory!" she shouted, then picked up her phone to text, only to find Jazz had started a group text with all the adults.

Jazz: "I'm with the security team looking at the footage."

Devin: "He's not at my car, and I've got my keys."

Marlie texted, "Anita's car and Jazz's car are here, and he's not with either of them."

Bri: "I'm at the door. We're phoning the family that just left."

"Cory!" came from a distance. That was Devin's voice, so Marlie ran toward him. When she reached him, he grabbed the jacket and started heading away. She called after him, "Where do you want me to look?"

He gestured vaguely behind her. "Check the garden paths near the pond. This way is the road, and I want to make sure he isn't trying to walk home."

Marlie headed toward the far end of the lot, unsure what she was even looking for, when it occurred to her to wonder why Cory would try heading home without his family.

It hit her then: because Cory wasn't heading "home."

Devin meant he was looking for his mother.

Without any sense of how the property was laid out, Marlie ran along the path in front of her. Fortunately it was made for people who had difficulty seeing and more difficulty walking, so it was wide and smooth. There wasn't ice yet, or else she'd have broken her neck. At some point, though, she stopped long enough to activate the phone's flashlight, then turn on her location for the other members of the group chat.

A gleam ahead told her she'd reached the pond. "Check the water first" was the advice she'd seen for whenever a child was missing, and even though Cory was unlikely to have waded into the pond, she stopped here.

"Cory!"

No response.

She checked the phone. The air was frigid against her hands, and she hoped it wouldn't drain her battery.

Bri: "We called the family. They didn't see Cory at all. He must have turned away from them as soon as he got out the door."

Jazz: "Security is still getting the footage up. Apparently they know how to set up cameras but not how to review them."

Brilliant.

Devin: "I'm on the road heading toward Main Street."

Anita: "I'm in my car. I'm going to drive about a mile up the road in the other direction."

Marlie texted, "Bri, go outside and circle the building heading left. I went out heading right."

Bri: "Got it."

Marlie didn't know how to think like a four-year-old. Cory had said he wanted to drive to find his mom, but then he'd been happy afterward. Happy...until he'd talked to Santa.

Marlie texted, "Jazz, talk to the guy who played Santa. Ask what Cory said to him."

Devin: "Good call. Something about that upset him."

Marlie kept walking, periodically shouting, "Cory!"

Bri: "Should we call the cops?"

Jazz: "The security guards are heading outside. They say they know how to find people."

Bri: "But they're not cops. We need an Amber alert."

Jazz: "Protocol is, if they can't find Cory in ten more minutes, they call the cops."

Marlie kept playing the dinner back in her head.

Cory, wanting a car to get his mother.

Cory, shocked that not everyone got Christmas presents.

Cory, wanting an accordion.

Cory, scared and sad while talking to Santa.

Cory, cutting snowflakes and folding cranes.

Cory, collecting all those cranes carefully into his bag.

By turns, Marlie could hear Bri calling from the other side of the building. "Cory!" Bri would call, and Marlie would wait half a minute, then call, "Cory!" on her side. In the frigid air, sound traveled. She and Bri had a building between them, but still their voices echoed to one another, a connection as they searched.

The phone vibrated in Marlie's hand. She raised it, wishing for gloves. Cory must be half frozen by now.

Jazz: "I have Santa here, and he remembered Cory."

Jazz: "He thought Cory was super scared of him, so he tried to be extra nice."

Jazz: "He said, 'Were you a good little boy?', and Cory got even more scared, so he said, 'Good little boys get presents, so I'm sure you'll get a lot.'"

Jazz: "Then he asked Cory what he wanted for Christmas, and Cory said he wanted a self-driving car."

Blast. The kid was trying to get to his mother. He didn't even know where she was, but he wanted to climb into his self-driving car and say, "Go find my mom."

Jazz: "Santa said, a car is too big, but is there something else you want? And he said Cory did tell him something after that, but he doesn't remember what it was."

Probably not an accordion. It must have been something so usual, so bland, that it didn't stick in Santa's mind.

Jazz: "Santa feels awful, by the way. I told him this isn't his fault."

Marlie called again, "Cory!"

Devin texted: "I just re-watched the video of the meeting with Santa. He was upset even before Santa told him about the car, so it wasn't just disappointment."

Anita: "I'm turning around and coming back. He wasn't on this part of the road."

Jazz: "They've got the security footage up. Cory ditched the family the second he got out the door and headed to the right, and then from there he went around the outside of the lot. The cameras don't get a reasonable shot of him again, but that means he didn't leave via the main entrance of the lot."

Devin: "Not that you saw."

Also Devin: "Mom just picked me up. We're going a bit further up toward Main and then turning back."

"Cory!" Where could he have gone? By now Marlie had left the pond behind, but the path branched. Keep going around the building? Or head off into the lawns? She scanned with her flashlight, but of course the beam didn't go far enough to show anything.

Cory wasn't wearing reflective clothing. She could pass within feet of him and not see. He'd been wearing sneakers and sweat pants and a long sleeve t-shirt, all dark. He wouldn't have his hat. The only light-colored, reflective thing would have been that plastic bag into which he'd scooped all those paper cranes.

Why the paper cranes? That was such an odd choice.

Marlie veered away from the building toward the woods.

Cory had avoided the adults in the parking lot the moment he could, so he'd probably avoid the building, too.

Paper cranes, protect this child.

Marlie gasped.

Paper cranes were supposed to protect him, so he'd taken them all. Except, what did he want them to protect him from?

Something gleamed in the flashlight, and Marlie stopped. It was the waxy coating of a crayoned paper crane.

She couldn't type with her fingers so cold. Instead, she dictated, "Guys, he was here! I found one of his paper cranes."

This time she ran. The property was huge, but Cory must be heading for the lights in that direction—a series of houses followed by the glow of Hartwell proper. She ran until the cold burned her lungs, every so often gasping, "Cory! Where are you?" and keeping her light trained on the ground in case he'd dropped any other cranes. Her phone was buzzing in her hands, but she didn't stop to check the screen because she was getting near the fence, and at the fence she saw something dark, and when she called, "Cory!" it moved toward her.

She aimed for him, and then he slammed into her, grasping her, sobbing, his skin cold to the touch. She pulled her arm out of her jacket sleeve and wrapped them in it together, then enclosed him in Devin's scarf. He cried in great jerking motions against her chest, and she squeezed him. Somehow she managed to hit the button to dictate into the chat, "I have him. He's okay. We're near a fence."

He'd almost gotten off the property. She tucked him up tighter under her jacket, then when she felt how he was shivering, she slipped herself out of the jacket entirely and zipped it around him.

"We were so scared," she said. "Why did you leave?"

He couldn't stop crying. Marlie dug in her jacket pockets to find a tissue, then cleaned the tears from his face, but he kept sobbing and shaking. She pulled him closer in case her body heat could warm him through the jacket. She should get him standing, but he was so upset, and she didn't know what to do.

Her phone buzzed.

Devin: "We're coming."

Bri: "Can you move him?"

Jazz: "Security's sending a car."

Marlie stayed put. She could see the road from where she was, and she listened for engine noise. She tried to rock him, hoping that would help a preschooler. "We were so worried. Where did you want to go?"

He gasped, "I don't want to go home. I can't. I don't want to. I don't want to."

"Why not?" She squeezed him. "What happened?"

He sobbed, "I'm not getting any presents. I don't want to go home and not get any presents, and everyone else is going to get presents, but Santa's not going to come, and I don't want to go home."

Marlie said, "You're going to get presents! You won't get a car, but you'll still get presents."

Cory pushed her away. "I haven't been good! I haven't been good, and he's not going to bring me anything! I never got anything before, and I'm not getting anything this year."

An engine sounded in the distance. Tears streaked Cory's face, and his mouth contorted into a frown. "I was so bad I made Mommy leave. I wasn't good for her, and Santa's not going to come, and I'm not going to get anything!"

"That's not true!" She held him tighter. "Cory, you're such a good boy. You're so good. Santa's going to give you presents!" but he sobbed even louder. "Cory, honey, your mom left because *she* was bad. Not because you were bad. Nothing you did could ever make her leave if she wanted to stay."

Everything Marlie was saying was all wrong, but Cory was so upset, and she had no idea what else to tell a boy who was convinced he'd destroyed his own world. She was just talking, wishing for the words that would calm him. "You're not bad. It's your mom's fault. You're lovable just as you are. Your grandma loves you, and Uncle Devin loves you, and I love you, and the fact that your mom didn't come back to you means she's broken inside. It means *she's* not getting presents from Santa, but you will. You could never be so bad that you'd deserve your mom to stop loving you."

Headlights swung through the circle at the end of the road, and Anita's car lurched to a halt. As the passenger door flung open, Marlie said, "Cory, believe me. Mothers are supposed to love their kids. Even when they're bad. Even when they do something really wrong."

Devin vaulted the fence with one hand on the top rail before sprinting the rest of the distance to them. "Cory! What in heaven's name were you doing?"

Marlie said, "Wait, Devin. He thinks he was bad. He thinks—"

Cory sobbed. The car door slammed as Anita rushed toward them.

Devin squatted in front of him, then pulled off his hat

and put it onto Cory's head. "What were you trying to do? Where were you going?"

His voice sounded desperate.

Marlie lowered her voice. "He thinks he was so bad that his mother left. He thinks Santa isn't going to give him any presents, because Santa only gives presents to good kids."

Cory was all-out shaking. Marlie cuddled him, and Devin lifted his chin with a finger. "Little Man. Little Man, look at me." When Cory met his gaze, mouth trembling, Devin said, "You're getting presents. Your presents are in the house right now. If you want, I will drive you home and show them to you."

Cory shook his head. Anita took him out of Marlie's lap and into her arms, but he was still looking at Devin.

Devin lowered his voice. "Your presents are in the house. You are a good kid, but even if you weren't a good kid, you'd be getting presents from Santa. And you're getting presents from me. And from Grandma."

Anita said, "Santa is a story. It's a fun story we're all supposed to enjoy, so you can have a Christmas surprise. The gifts from Santa actually come from us. We bought your presents. They're all wrapped up at home, waiting for you."

Cory clung to her. The security vehicle had pulled into the circle as well, but Anita said to Devin, "Get him in the car. He needs to warm up."

Devin hefted him up right from the ground. Anita said to Marlie, "You're cold."

She didn't even feel it anymore. She was completely numb.

Anita sat in the car with the engine running and the heat blasting. Cory didn't get into his car seat, just stayed beside

Marlie in the back with a blanket over them both. He whispered, "Santa is just pretend?"

Anita said, "Santa is a story we tell little kids because it's fun. It's an excuse to buy you special toys. When kids get big, then we tell them that it was their family buying gifts all along, and we all get to keep playing the game for the littler kids."

Cory frowned, and Marlie pulled him tighter.

Devin was outside talking to the security people. With shaking hands, Marlie texted Jazz and Bri, "We're in the car," and then, "It was Santa after all. Cory thought he wasn't a good boy."

But he was.

Devin got into the car, and Marlie shivered, but not with the cold.

Chapter Seventeen

Santa met Cory at the front door of the Willowgate, in full Santa gear. Anita brought Cory up to Santa, and Cory hugged him, then whispered, "I know your secret."

Santa nodded solemnly. "But we won't tell the little kids? We'll keep the surprise for them, too?" When Cory agreed, Santa said, "Even if Santa was real, you would get presents. You are a very good boy."

They took Cory home, all but Devin. It wasn't fair, but Devin still needed to finish out his shift, clean the kitchen, and do the occasional short-order-cookery. Before they left, he said to Marlie, "Thank you for finding him."

She couldn't meet his eyes. "It was a group effort."

He'd taken his scarf from Cory but didn't give it back to her. That only made sense.

At home, Anita made everyone hot chocolate, but then Jazz took over and told Anita to go watch a Christmas show with her grandson. The two of them cuddled on the couch, and eventually Marlie went downstairs to the finished basement. She texted her parents and her brother, "Merry Christmas Eve."

They didn't reply. She didn't expect them to.

Still uncertain, Cory asked to see his presents, so Anita brought in the box from the garage. "You can't open them yet," she said, "but these will all be here for you in the morning."

Cory beamed.

Anita added, "And you cannot wake up at four in the morning to open them alone."

He frowned, but she said, "Really. You are not to open your gifts without all of us awake."

Anita stayed alongside Cory while he went to sleep. Jazz finally got a chance to talk with her husband. Bri tucked herself up on the couch to read by the tree, and Marlie sat in the kitchen folding paper cranes.

Sat thinking.

Thinking a lot, in fact.

I wish.

She'd said to Cory, "Nothing you did could ever make her leave if she wanted to stay."

How true was that?

Was it always true?

When Anita had heard that Marlie's parents were abandoning for the holiday, had she stepped in as a mom because she knew what a mother ought to do?

Marlie had so much to explain to Devin. But first, she had so much to explain to herself.

———————

At eleven o'clock, Devin's car idled for a while in the driveway. It was an hour until Christmas.

All Cory's presents were arranged under the tree, as well

as some presents for Devin. Also, despite the ban on presents for adults, bad Anita had bought gifts for her three guests.

Jazz and Bri had gone to bed. Anita was asleep as well, although for the life of her, Marlie wasn't sure how she'd resisted sleeping on the floor of Cory's room.

As for herself, Marlie sat at the table in her oversized flannel pajamas, with an entire origami nativity scene arranged before her. The instructions hadn't been hard to find, but they'd been hard to follow. Still, one fold at a time, she'd formed a tiny family.

Creased paper wanted to follow the grooves already made for itself. If you creased it incorrectly, it didn't want to go back into another groove.

The same could be said for people.

Eventually, Devin entered the kitchen, then sighed when he saw Marlie. "Really? You should have gone to bed. Haven't we had enough excitement for one holiday?"

"You did say it wasn't an exciting Christmas until the cops were called, and, well, we got that." Marlie shook her head. "I owe you an apology and an explanation."

Without taking off his coat, Devin leaned in the doorframe. "And?"

He wasn't going to join her. Marlie said, "Before you got to Cory, I was trying to talk him down off the ledge because he was so upset. But what I was saying to him—I think it was all the stuff I needed to hear."

Devin frowned. "Go on. You were telling him he wasn't a bad little boy who deserved coal in his stocking, and therefore you thought I might not be a bad little boy who didn't deserve coal, either?"

His eyes were dark, and he looked exhausted.

"My problem wasn't with you. It was never with you, and I'm sorry I made you feel judged." Marlie stared at her folded hands. "Cory thought he'd been so bad that his mother didn't love him. I kept telling him he was lovable. If Rachel doesn't want to be with him, the problem is her, not him."

Devin nodded. "That was the right thing to say."

"The thing is, all my life, I knew love was something I had to earn. I had to earn it with good behavior, and then, to keep that love, I had to make maintenance payments by doing things like getting good grades, obeying, looking pretty, and being quiet." She took a deep breath. "Part of those payments, the way to earn approval, was only dating people my mother would consider acceptable to her."

Devin opened his hands. "Enter the criminal mischief-maker."

Marlie snorted. "Enter the car thief! But after reassuring Cory, I realized, that's nonsense. My mother's love is conditional. My father couldn't be bothered with me no matter how good I was, and my mother always set litmus tests, and then if I passed, she set another, harder test. If Cory thought he wasn't getting presents because he was a bad boy, then even more than that, I wasn't getting love because I was a disappointment of a daughter."

Devin scowled, but it wasn't directed at her. "How dare she?"

"You were always a light in my world, I think because you did what you wanted. You never worried about what other people thought of you." Marlie looked away again, but she couldn't hide her smile. "It was intoxicating. You were fearless about loving and about being loved. Your mother loved you when you climbed out the window and when you set fire to the Christmas display and when you just up and left school at lunch and walked home because you felt like it."

Devin said, "I did *not* set fire to the Christmas display." He hesitated. "Not intentionally."

"You were freedom and amazement and wonder. It never concerned you whether you were acceptable to anyone else, and I felt this vicarious thrill every time I watched you." Marlie shook her head. "I crushed so hard on you, but I was fifteen. I couldn't take my mother's disapproval if I dated the car thief, or really anyone she didn't think was going to make her look like an amazing mother."

Devin approached the table and sat across from Marlie. "So, you're saying, your mother's breaking up with me?"

"I'm telling you, I'm breaking up with my mother's expectation. When Mrs. Addison was talking, I didn't hear condemnation of *you*. I heard condemnation of *me*. What I realized doesn't absolve me, but it helps me understand exactly how and why I mistreated you." It was difficult, but Marlie looked into Devin's eyes. "In her disapproval and in Shirley's, I heard echoes of what my mother would say. But why should I care? Why should I keep scrambling for approval she's never going to give? It's what I said to Cory. My mother's inability to love me is my mother's fault, not mine. I should never have had to earn that."

Devin's fists clenched. "That makes sense. You shouldn't."

Marlie blinked hard. "I'm sorry I made you think you weren't good enough. You have always been good enough, and you will always be good enough, and if anything, you're better than good enough."

Devin folded his arms. "Even if I steal the occasional road

sign?"

Marlie gestured with one hand. "Unpaved trenches behind. Everything's been paved over, and your road is smooth."

He gestured at the table. "And the origami?"

"I made a whole origami nativity scene, and I think it came pretty nice." Marlie picked up one of the lambs. "But here's the thing—origami is all about folding the paper up and changing its shape so it looks like something it's not." She picked up a triangle into which she'd cut a few notches, but which she hadn't unfolded yet. "A paper snowflake is the opposite, where you unfold it to show what it's truly become."

She unfolded the snowflake so he could see all the frosty spines, saying, "I've been living like an origami figure, folded up to be something for someone else, collapsing along the creases someone else pressed. But those creases aren't in the right places. I came to your home thinking it was an origami Christmas." She pivoted the snowflake in her hands. "But you turned it into a paper snowflake Christmas."

He reached across the table for her.

She took his hand, then looked up. "Will you accept my apology?"

He said, voice low, "Apology accepted."

It was a start. She didn't deserve even that much, but at least tomorrow wouldn't be awkward.

He squeezed her fingers. "What are you going to do about your mother?"

"I don't know. I may try to talk to her about it."

He said, "And your father? Who presumably has let this go on for your entire life and therefore is in agreement with her treatment?"

She shook her head. "Him, too. And—I don't know how they're going to take that."

"You have everything to be proud of. You're smart, and you're doing what you love. You have awesome hobbies." Devin paused. "You make awesome friends."

Marlie smiled. "I do, don't I?"

Devin said, "For example, Jazz. She's your longest friend, and she looks out for you."

Marlie nodded. "And Bri. She definitely has my back."

Devin said, "My mother's always liked you."

Marlie drummed her fingers on the table. "Now...is there anyone else?"

Devin frowned in thought. "I'm sure there must be, if only we could think of someone." He stood from the table. "Grab your jacket and come with me."

Marlie gestured to her flannel pajamas. He said, "We won't go far."

When she'd pulled on her boots and her jacket, they got in the SUV. It was still warm from his drive home, but he handed her the blanket from the back. She buckled in, then tucked it around herself. They hadn't been on the road a full minute before the wipers swished over the windshield.

She sat forward. "Is it snowing?"

"A bit." It wasn't supposed to be. Devin took a couple of turns away from the main road, and then brought them into a subdivision with all the houses lit up. "Because of Cory's stunt, you didn't get to see the lights tonight, and I know you wanted to."

They crawled through the side streets, winding through the identical townhomes, then through the older houses with their assortments of additions and bump-outs, finally the residential neighborhoods where the homes had marginal differences, but every lawn had a pine tree and two azalea bushes. They stopped in front of a home with lights outlining every facet, and beside it a home with exactly one strand of blinking lights tossed over a bush.

They pulled in at the town park, the lot empty and the crowds departed, but the exhibits still lit. "Come on, Pajama Girl," he said, and she wrapped the blanket over her jacket as they left the toasty vehicle. They walked through the exhibits again, then stopped at the pond where the path was still arched over with lights.

Their breath frosted up between them, and when Marlie raised her face to his, she felt tiny sparkles of snowflakes against her cheeks. "You've made it a wonderful Christmas for me."

She wrapped the blanket around them both, and he held her beneath the lights.

She said, "Can we give this a shot? If I promise to accept you for who you are—past, present, and future—then can you accept me, too?"

He pulled her closer, then smiled. "I'd like that very much. Merry Christmas."

He kissed her, and the lights went out.

Marlie snickered. He muttered, "Of course."

She snuggled closer to him. "I expect nothing less."

"So absolutely rude to turn them off at midnight." He snorted. "But then again, that means no one can see me kissing you again."

She raised her arms around his shoulders and pulled him closer. "Turn on all the lights in the world if you want. I don't care if everyone sees."

CHAPTER EIGHTEEN

"Merry Christmas!"

Marlie tried to ignore the pounding on the door and the shrieking voice of a four-year-old, followed by the guest room door slamming open and the knob banging into the wall. "It's Christmas!"

The lights flared on overhead.

"Cory!" That hissed reprimand was Anita. "Don't wake everyone!"

As the lights went back off and the door closed, Marlie heard a muffled, "But you said not to open presents until everyone was awake!"

From the bed, Bri mumbled, "That kid should be a lawyer."

"I know, right?" Jazz stretched in bed. "Perfect adherence to the letter of the law, and completely missing what it means."

Marlie checked her phone. It was five-fifteen.

A shriek of joy confirmed that Marlie ought to actually

get up. "I guess we're doing this."

In the entrance of the living room, Cory was leaping in place. "It's a blizzard!"

Paper snowflakes filled the living room. They hung from threads affixed to the ceiling, were taped to the walls, and had been scattered over the Christmas tree. More dangled from the entranceway. They lay atop the presents and on the couches and coffee table.

Turning toward Marlie, Anita grinned. "You did all this?"

Marlie folded her arms and cocked her head. "Maybe. Maybe I had a little help from your troublemaker son."

Footsteps trudged up the steps. "Be careful when you say my name. I might show up."

Cory ran to Devin. "You're up. That means presents! And look at all the snowflakes."

"Wow, almost like I put them there." Devin picked him up. "When it snows on Christmas, they call it a white Christmas, and we thought you should have one even though it didn't really snow."

"Oh for crying out loud," mumbled a bleary-eyed Jazz, leaning against the wall. "Did you two spend the whole night doing this?"

Marlie's cheeks flushed. "Well, we didn't want Cory to be disappointed for his first real Christmas."

Devin said, "Marlie turned into a pumpkin at around three-thirty, but we had most of it done by then. She was cutting, and I was hanging."

A significant portion of snowflakes had hearts on them. That must have been where Marlie's mind was hovering last night.

Anita said, "Well, I hope you enjoyed *both* hours of sleep, because Christmas Day has begun."

Anita set the cinnamon rolls in the oven, and then they sat around the besnowed living room while Cory ripped open his gifts. Every single present was the best present anyone had ever given anybody, including when he opened a sweater and a stack of books. He also got a train set, an assortment of die-cast cars, some puzzles, and a plush piggy as big as he was, with a card signed from Jazz, Bri, and Marlie.

"We got it yesterday while we were shopping," Bri whispered to Marlie. "The second Jazz saw that monstrosity, there was no way we were leaving the store without it."

Devin got more subdued gifts, and gave more subdued thank-yous (to be expected when compared to the geyser of thank-you erupting at his side). Bri, Jazz, and Marlie each got gift bags with a throw blanket, fuzzy socks, and a scented candle. Devin had given Anita new slippers, kitchen shears (which for some reason she loved,) two sweaters, and a memoir by her favorite actress.

After cinnamon rolls for breakfast, with Devin needing to get to work by two, he managed to grab a quick nap so he wouldn't fall asleep in the middle of grilling one of the residents a hamburger. Anita got to work cooking, with Jazz and Marlie helping.

During a lull, Marlie sent photos to her parents. She periodically checked the chat window, and when she saw the status switch to "read," she hit the button to call. Dad didn't answer. Mom did.

"Hey. Merry Christmas." Marlie's voice was soft. "How's the wedding?"

"Oh, it was amazing. I'll need to send you pictures." Mom then launched on a description of the bridal gown, the ceremony, the flowers, the five-course dinner, the music, the speeches, the bridesmaid dresses, the bride's engagement ring, and the mother of the bride dress.

Marlie said, "We went to a Christmas party last night."

"Oh, that's lovely! So sorry, honey, but I need to go to the post-wedding breakfast now. I'm glad you called. Merry Christmas!"

In the kitchen, Anita checked the temperature on their Christmas ham while Jazz cut up potatoes and Cory assembled a plastic garage for his cars. Christmas music played on the television, and the gas fireplace was lit, casting moving lights on the paper snowflakes dotting the living room.

Her parents had made a choice for an opulent Christmas with all the bragging rights, but Marlie preferred what Devin had right here: expansive love that never had to fold itself up small so it could look like something else.

Before Devin went to work, Marlie intercepted him at the door holding an origami cube.

He gave her a devilish grin. "And this is?"

"I may have made a present for you." Marlie proffered it on the tip of one finger.

Devin mock-frowned. "Do I recall incorrectly that we had agreed on no presents?"

"Maybe." Marlie pinched it between thumb and forefinger and raised it up. "Aren't you remotely curious?"

"Maybe I am." He plucked it from her. "It also feels curiously hollow."

She shrugged. "Perhaps there's something inside."

"Perhaps there is." He tucked it into his pocket. "Well, thank you."

She stepped into his way as he attempted to move toward the door. "Aren't you going to open it?"

"I prefer the anticipation." He arched his brows. "The sweetness of wondering, the tantalizing mystery—"

Marlie folded her arms.

He opened his hands. "What can I say?"

She reached up with her arms around his neck. "You could say, Merry Christmas."

"I could say that." He lowered his forehead to hers. "Maybe you could say something, too."

Marlie whispered, "Maybe what I have to say is inside the cube."

"Ooh." He nuzzled her ear, sending chills along her throat. "Now that is quite certainly a tantalizing mystery."

He kissed her neck, then kissed her jawline, and then she turned so he could kiss her lips. "Merry Christmas," he breathed.

He released her, then stepped toward the door.

Marlie said, "You're really not going to open it?"

"You know me. I'm an inveterate troublemaker." He winked at her, mischief in his eyes. "But I'll be back tonight, and maybe then you can tell me what's inside."

Epilogue

The first graders' Alphabet Parade on the afternoon before winter break was a Hartwell tradition, but Marlie didn't remember it being quite this frigid.

"You're remembering wrong," Anita said. "When you and Devin were in first grade, it was far colder, and it was raining."

Devin joined them. "I've managed to keep Cory from leading the parade out before the teacher was ready for them to go." He looked back at the gym doors, more than a little concerned. "I think."

Marlie took his gloved hand in hers. "He wouldn't be your nephew if he didn't try something like that for the occasion."

Murmuring, "As if I didn't already have enough grey hairs," Anita got out her phone and opened the camera. "I'm going to get closer so I at least have a photo of whatever he does."

Cory had been assigned the letter F, and he'd chosen to parade as "Family." He'd found a baby doll to carry as he marched with his letter sign.

With his fingers intertwined with Marlie's, Devin slipped

both their hands into his pocket. Marlie said, "I don't remember if you did anything wild at our Christmas Alphabet Parade."

"Mr. Pendergast put me in a harness and buggy shafts, and made me the letter R so I had to go as Rudolph." Devin frowned. "I convinced the kid with the letter S, going as the sleigh, to run like crazy so maybe we could fly, and the poor kid with the letter P ran after us because he was the presents."

By contrast, Marlie had been J, for Joy, and had walked the length of the parade—all the way from the gym door to the cafeteria door—blowing bubbles, to polite applause.

The gym doors opened, and the first teachers walked outside, each holding a letter on a pole. M was Mrs. Claus, followed by S, a teacher decked out in sparkly white, trailing long gauzy scarves, who was clearly Snow.

"I hear no screaming," Devin said. "So far, so good."

Marlie said, "Are there normally screams?"

Devin said, "If I ever lose track of him at the playground, I look for parents staring in shock, surreptitiously reaching for their cell phones so they can call 911 that much faster. I walk the way they're facing, and that's how I find Cory. Every time."

Marlie bit her lip. "You know that curse about having a kid just like you?"

"He's not even my kid." Devin shuddered. "But speaking of kids, here they come."

The Alphabet Parade began in earnest. P for Presents. E for Elf. T for Tree. All good so far. And then, from the far end of the parade, erupted loud laughter and shouting.

Devin muttered, "Incoming Cory detected."

About to say, "You don't know that for sure," Marlie

stopped herself. Then, as the tumult drew closer, she did, in fact, see Cory.

Cory, brandishing a pole with the letter F, was hurling candy out into the crowd. He shouted, "I'm *Festive!*"

Devin snatched a candy out of the air as it sailed past his head. "Oh for crying out loud—this is his Halloween candy!"

Marlie said, "He saved it two months for this?" She lowered her voice. "You've got to give him credit for his determination."

"He snuck it out of the house in his backpack, too, the rascal. He told me he was using a baby doll he'd found in one of my sisters' rooms." Devin grimaced. "You know..."

Marlie picked up a lollipop from the ground. "At least it's tasty mischief, and nothing's on fire."

After the parade ended, everyone went inside for watery hot chocolate and an unhealthy amount of noise. Marlie looked around hoping someone had turned up as E for Earplugs, but instead it was V for Volume.

Cory bounced over, wielding a popcorn ball. "F is for *funny!*"

Devin folded his arms. "F is for *fuss formed by flinging fifty fistfuls of confections*, and I'm going to get one of those special calls from the school again, aren't I?"

Marlie said, "Does it warm your heart when you sound just like your mother?" and Devin flinched.

Cory said to Marlie, "Did you like your present?"

Devin said, "What? Cory—no."

"I love the origami box for you that he made!" Cory jumped in place. "He watched a video and I made a box too, but he put your present inside his, and he told me it was a secret so I couldn't talk to you about it until after he gave it to you, but since it wasn't a Christmas present, he was going to give it to you today."

Marlie said to Cory, "Did he tell you *when* today he was giving it to me?"

Cory frowned as he thought. "No."

Devin pretended to put his hands on Cory's neck. "I didn't give it to her yet, you little weasel."

He said, "Oh," and then, "F is for *fleeing*." He dashed off into the crowd of kids.

Shaking his head, Devin said, "M for Murder wouldn't be in the Christmas spirit, would it?"

Marlie said, "I'm good with C for Convenient Amnesia, though."

Devin reached into his jacket pocket. "Well, after all the origami you've made, I did want to try making some, myself."

He pulled out an origami cube, about an inch along each side, just like the one Marlie had made him. She said, "You did a good job!"

When she held it, though, it was heavier than just paper. She shook it, but it didn't rattle.

Marlie arched her eyebrows. "So—what did you fill this with?"

Devin shrugged. "You'll have to open it to find out."

She shook it again. "Is it full of gunpowder, like those Christmas crackers? No, wait, you were doing this with Cory in the room." She held it up to her ear. "It's not ticking. Maybe I should ask Cory if it's safe to open. He'll tell me."

"I bet he would." Devin scanned the room as though uninterested in the proceedings. "But then you won't have a surprise."

"You're always surprising." She shook it again. "You never open any of my cubes, so maybe I shouldn't open this one, either."

Grinning, Devin met her eyes. "That would be a valid choice, yes."

"You're infuriating. I can't get any kind of rise out of you." Marlie started slipping the edges of the cube apart, and the box unfolded to reveal a diamond solitaire taped to the paper.

"You said you were more of a paper snowflake than an origami crane." Devin took her hand. "But in the past two years, you've unfolded more of your heart to me, and I've taken shape with you. Will you marry me and make every Christmas a paper snowflake Christmas?"

Marlie slipped the ring onto her hand, then put her arms around him. "I love you." She kissed him, then pressed her cheek against his shoulder. "Yes, I will marry you."

THANK YOU!

Thank you so much for reading about Marlie and Devin! It's so much fun to write about your friendly neighborhood troublemaker—especially in a small town where everyone knows everyone else, so little trouble becomes big trouble.

If you loved the story, please consider leaving a review over at Goodreads or wherever you purchased it. Reviews help other readers, and they help me, too. It doesn't have to be a book report, just a star rating and a couple of sentences about what you liked or didn't like. I really appreciate when readers take the time to do this.

Thank you to Julie Monette for her editing work, Christine Murphy of Paper or Pixels for the fun cover, and all the troublemakers in my life who contributed their mischief to this story.

Please join me for **Maddie Mondays**. Every Monday, I try to send a short email with a vignette about life in swampy small-town New England, as well as a recommendation for something—a book, a knitting pattern, or anything else I think you'll find interesting. You can do that at **https://stats.sender.net/forms/erBXBe/view**

Thanks once more, and until we meet again, keep reading!

ALSO BY MADDIE EVANS...

If you liked Devin as a troublemaker, have I got a pair for you. In *Beach Wedding on the Rocks,* Noah and Elsie are invited to the wedding of the man whose prank broke up their relationship. Well, turnabout is fair play, is it not?

As Elsie and Noah plan (and pull off!) a series of hilarious stunts, though, the old feelings and questions flood back like a tide over the rocks. What begins as a pact to get payback turns into a week of missteps, mixed signals, and misguided attempts to deny everything that's kept them apart for so long.

These two just look like trouble, don't they?

ALSO FROM PHILANGELUS PRESS...

Three nights before Christmas, with the temperatures below zero and falling, Officer Kevin Farrell finds three homeless children in a bus station. He brings them to the safest place he can think of: his brother Jay's church.

Jay is a disabled priest. Kevin hasn't spoken to Jay for years because Kevin can't believe in God after all the evil he's seen.

To save the kids, they'll have to work together. To work together, they'll have to mend the rift between them.

Both men think their brotherhood irreparably broken, but Christmas is the season of second chances.